MY NAME IS REVENGE

A novella and collected essays

by

ASHLEY KALAGIAN BLUNT

Spineless Wonders
PO Box 220
STRAWBERRY HILLS
New South Wales, Australia, 2012
shortaustralianstories.com.au

First published by Spineless Wonders 2019
Text copyright © remains with the author
Cover image and design by Imogen Rowe for Bettina Kaiser Art & Design

Edited by Bronwyn Mehan with editorial assistance by Bridgette Sulicich
Layout by Bettina Kaiser Art & Design

Typeset in Baskerville
Printed and bound by Ingram Spark
ISBN 978-1-925052-44-2

My Name Is Revenge
A novella and collected essays/Ashley Kalagian Blunt

Distribution in Australia and New Zealand by New South

A catalogue record for this book is available from the National Library of Australia

Praise for *My Name Is Revenge*

A heartfelt and gripping story of family, hardship and resilience.
> – *Candice Fox, bestselling author of* Crimson Lake

Ashley Kalagian Blunt weaves a mostly-forgotten strand of our history into a compelling contemporary crime story. *My Name Is Revenge* manages to be both unflinching in its depiction of inherited hatreds and compassionate about the experience of living with the terrible aftermath of a genocide that the world has largely ignored.
> – *Emily Maguire, author of* An Isolated Incident

Informed by a passion to express the haunting of almost unimaginable historical crimes, and the tragic shapes that vengeance for those crimes can take. … Kalagian Blunt expertly and compassionately examines the nature of truth and its representation via the conjunction of fiction and essay.
> – *Carmel Bird, Patrick White Literary Award winner*

Kalagian Blunt has written a Molotov cocktail of a book. Her work explodes with urgency on every page, calling us to recognise deep historical injustices and atrocities, inflicted on the Armenian people but touching us all; and it flames with her storytelling talent.
> – *Lee Kofman, author of* The Dangerous Bride

Ashley Kalagian Blunt delivers what truly potent novellas are capable of: awakening us to new possibilities of thought and feeling. As with Orwell's *Animal Farm* and Garner's *The Children's Bach*, this story raises questions that linger and does not give us easy answers. Raw, intense and at times unbearably tender, Kalagian Blunt gives voice to survivors of the Armenian genocide – voices that cry out to be heard in their power and poignancy, their historic hurts and continuing hope for redemption.
> – *Katerina Cosgrove, author of* Bone Ash Sky

An imaginative work of fiction and a work reflecting upon history … a fine example of why history matters and why we should be pushed to reconsider assumptions about how history was and how it might be understood.

> – *Peter Stanley, co-author of* Armenia, Australia & the Great War

My Name Is Revenge is a fascinating and expertly crafted story based on a little-known event in Australia's history. In the compelling novella, Kalagian Blunt handles this sensitive topic with empathy and an impressive attention to detail, drawing the reader in with intriguing characters and a strong sense of place. The accompanying essay brings to life the struggles faced by Armenians and their children as they strived to be accepted by their adopted homelands, while governments sought to erase evidence of the atrocities committed against the Armenian population. The two separate but linked pieces of literature come together to pose an important and difficult question to readers: Can violence ever be justified?

> – *Amanda Ortlepp, author of* Claiming Noah

Against a backdrop of eucalypts and thrumming cicadas, Kalagian Blunt deftly sketches her portrait of a family reckoning with its past. In her interweaving of Australian and Armenian histories, Kalagian Blunt illustrates and animates just how intricately linked her forebears' past is with Australia's own. Dealing imaginatively with questions of radicalisation, displacement, and assimilation, this story feels very pertinent to our current political climate, and makes for a gripping read.

> – *Adele Dumont, author of* No Man Is an Island

… A moving and informative piece of writing. Its history lesson is worthwhile, but even more so is its exploration of family, community and outsiders. It's about the way that denial doesn't solve a thing in life, and acknowledgment of the past is the very least that we owe our forebears.

> – *Karen Chisholm,* Newtown Review of Books

For Mariam and Paravon

My Name Is Revenge

A novella

On 17 December 1980, at 9:47 am, two men shot the Turkish consul-general to Sydney and his bodyguard near the consul's home in Vaucluse. The assassins aimed, fired and vanished.

Vrezh was home the morning of 17 December, across the harbour at 29 Whiting Street, Lane Cove, that quiet, leafy Lower North Shore suburb. The lab's holiday shutdown meant he could sleep in, sticky with sweat, a single sheet tangled around his knees. Through the parted curtains, a laser blast of sun reached the edge of his pillow. The ceiling fan beat the heavy summer air.

He woke to his mother shouting in Armenian. Pulling on a t-shirt, Vrezh stumbled out of the twin bed where he'd slept since their first night at 29 Whiting Street, down the thickly carpeted stairs, through the dark wood and tufted leather sofas of the lounge, watched by the five sets of eyes of the family oil portrait on the far wall, and into the kitchen.

The assassination was on the radio.

'What are they saying, Vrezh? Who are they saying is responsible?' His mother forgot all her English when she got flustered, and now she had one hand thrusting toward the radio, the other clamped to the side of her face. She wore her apron, sleeves rolled up, her hair in rollers. The kitchen smelt of ground lamb and onion. Vrezh's grandfather Arshag, his father's father, sat at the table, a tiny cup of coffee in front of him, a blanket around his shoulders.

The baritone newsreader's voice hit Vrezh like adrenaline.

'What is it, Vrezh, I cannot understand!' his mother shouted again.

'The Justice Commandos of the Armenian Genocide – a woman called the station, claiming it was them.' Vrezh focused on translating the announcer's words, struggling to smother his excitement. 'The caller said the attack was retaliation for the injustices done to the Armenians.'

His mother removed her glasses and pressed her palms into her eyes. Held them there while the newsreader moved on to other stories.

'My good Lord. This terrible violence that never ends.'

Then came the metallic *brrrrriiiinnnggg* of the phone. Vrezh's father, calling from the jewellery store. Wanting to know if they'd heard.

'Publicly we must call this a deplorable crime,' his father said, his voice lowered.

Vrezh murmured his understanding. Like his father, he had followed the actions of the Justice Commandos and ASALA, the Armenian Secret Army for the Liberation of Armenia, since their start five years earlier. Attacks against

Turkish diplomats in LA, Athens, Paris, Beirut, Madrid. Today they had finally reached Sydney.

For the first time, Vrezh felt empowered.

From the corridor where the phone hung against a wallpaper of yellow and orange flowers, Vrezh could see into the kitchen. His mother bending over the stovetop, tasting the meat for the *kufteh*. His grandfather's shaky hand reaching for his coffee, the cup slipping from his fingers, the brown liquid running in rivulets over the rust-orange plastic tablecloth, dripping onto the floor. And the absence of his brother, Armen, the one person he burned to speak to.

With his forearms wide and heavy on the table, his thick shoulders and full head of coal black waves combed back, Vrezh's father presided over platters piled with roast eggplant, capsicum and lamb skewers.

'Where is your brother tonight?'

Armen still wasn't home. Vrezh shrugged, eyes on his plate. 'Out with Gavik and Vartan. Where else?'

Where else?

His mother leafed through the day's letters while they ate. Here and there, she read a bit of news aloud, from Vrezh's aunt in Boston, his uncle in Moscow, his grandmother – his mother's mother, still in Egypt. Their family, scattered like ashes across the earth. As a child, Vrezh had imagined his family one day reuniting in Armenia. What was this 'Soviet Union' that was so powerful it could prevent them from living in their homeland? Now he envied the uncomplicated naivety of childhood.

Alone in his bedroom, Vrezh spread every newspaper article about the assassination across his desk. Holding a magnifying glass over photos from the scene, he analysed where the shooter might have stood, how the motorcyclist likely manoeuvred along the residential streets to escape. He checked weather reports, considered wind resistance, the angle of the sun's glint on that too-bright morning. He read and re-read the scant police statements.

None of it revealed what he really wanted to know.

Later, Vrezh fell asleep on the burgundy lounge sofa, two tasselled cushions under his head. The lounge was adjacent to his grandfather's makeshift bedroom. His father had sacrificed his office when the stairs became too difficult for Arshag's arthritic knees and doddering steps. In recent weeks, Vrezh had been sleeping in the lounge more often, giving his mother a break.

Weak-throated shouts roused him. He ran the few steps to his grandfather's room.

'The Turks! They're coming for me!' Arshag's hoarse shouts were an echo of terror across a chasm of six decades. One foot on the floor, the other tangled in sheets. Naked arms fought something unseen.

'Grandfather, it's Vrezh.' He repeated this, trying to steady the old man before he fell and shattered a hip. His mother's fear – that Arshag would die in a hospital surrounded by indifferent strangers. *They will put him in a straight jacket again, Vrezh. It is a like a prison for him!* Vrezh remembered the jacket, hung on a hook beside the hospital bed, its three oversized buckles used to trap the arms. They restrained him at night, his mother explained, so he couldn't hurt himself. Still, it was unbearable to her. *Better he is with family*, she repeated.

Now Arshag lay on the bed in his room, lamplight catching the skeletal edges of his cheeks. His bulging eyes stared at the ceiling. Sinking into the armchair, Vrezh kept a hand on his grandfather's forearm, squeezing, as if to transfer his energy into the old man's withered muscles, his terrified face.

*

The cup teetered on the table's edge, for a moment looking as though it might not fall. Vrezh reached back to it, but it fell, bouncing, splashing water across the linoleum.

'Look at this mess!' Arshag's arms flung wide, his eyeballs about to pop out of their sockets.

Vrezh jumped back. His scrawny fingers gripped the edge of his grandmother's apron. He was as tall as her hip.

'It's only water.' Seda pulled a cloth from her apron pocket, leaning to the floor.

'Encouraging him! He needs to toughen up!' Arshag shouted as he stalked out the back door, slamming it, a breath of dusty Cairo air blown in behind him.

'Sorry, *tatik*.' Vrezh's eyes welled and he swiped at them with his shirtsleeves, afraid his grandfather would crash back through the door like a bull to call him a snivelling baby.

Seda wiped his nose with the bottom corner of her apron, then returned to her chair and the bucket of peas on the table. Vrezh settled on a stool by her feet, still snuffling, holding a smaller bowl of peas on his lap.

'Do you know that when your grandfather was your age, his father went missing?' Her voice remained calm as she separated peas from pods. 'They lived in a town called Erzurum, in Anatolia. His mother cried for two days. Then there was a knock on the door, late at night.'

Vrezh's hands dropped the peas. He searched his grand-mother's face, saw nothing unusual there. Yet he tensed, sensing something shift in the room.

'Turkish soldiers. They tore apart everything in the house. Your grandfather stood with his mother and brother at the front door. He had a little brother, did you know that?'

Vrezh shook his head.

'His mother shouted at the Turks. They hit her with their guns. The soldiers made all the Armenians in the town leave, right then, in the middle of the night. They started walking, hundreds of people, the Turks on their horses, snapping their whips to make the Armenians walk faster.'

Vrezh was still shaking his head, as if this might stop his grandmother from saying any more. If he stood to press a hand to her lips, his fingers would come away with the rosy lipstick she always wore, he knew. But he stayed pinned to his stool.

'In the town square, a row of men were hanging from ropes. In the moonlight, your grandfather could see his father's face.

'They kept walking, into the desert. They had almost no food. One night his mother vanished. He searched for her, asking the other Armenians. No-one answered him. He held his little brother's hand tight, kept him right at his side. But his brother started crying. The Turks shouted at him, but he wouldn't be quiet.'

Vrezh wanted his grandmother to stop now. Stop. That was enough.

'His brother cried and cried. Finally, the soldiers stopped him. A group of women dragged your grandfather away, forced him to keep walking. For days his brother's cries echoed in his ears. He still hears them.'

Seda's voice remained as steady as if she was listing the items they would buy at the market that afternoon. She peered over her glasses, into his eyes.

'When your grandfather shouts, it's not about you. He's shouting about his father and mother, and the little boy who was his brother. You understand?'

Vrezh gave one quick, tiny nod.

'The Turks say none of this happened.' Seda's hands were finally still. 'They want the whole world to forget. You and Armen, you must not forget.'

*

Vrezh ignored the engineering papers piled on his desk. It had been twenty-four hours since the assassination. Things were happening that mattered much more than his spectroscopic analysis research.

His mother was out, no-one else home except Arshag, asleep in the lounge room. Vrezh headed down the hall to Armen's bedroom.

They'd moved to Sydney, to this house, when he was eight. The city so empty, so quiet compared to Cairo, the sky so wide and blue. When their father announced that the new house was large enough for the boys to have separate bedrooms, Vrezh swallowed the feeling of abandonment. He parroted Armen's relief.

Why don't we live in Armenia? Vrezh asked his father as they sliced through the packing tape on box after box at 29 Whiting Street, Lane Cove.

The Turks stole our homes and murdered our families. But one day, Vrezh, we will take back our homeland.

There was no lock on Armen's bedroom door – you don't lock yourself away from your family, their father decreed. Inside Armen's room, however, were many locks. On his desk drawers, on the trunk at the foot of his single bed, and on a carved wooden box he kept under the closet floorboards.

When he started staying out longer, staying away for days, Armen, with his loud politics, his militant attitude, had also gone strangely quiet. Something had changed, something unspoken. Vrezh questioned his brother, paid close attention. Armen revealed nothing.

Now, this shooting.

Vrezh opened the blinds above his brother's bed a few centimetres. Heat radiated off the glass. Bottles of cologne cut a straight line across the top of Armen's dresser, labels facing front. Clothes stacked like they were on sale at David Jones, shoes gleaming. Armen insisted Mother iron even his socks. She obliged – she was an Armenian mother – though she nagged him to get married already, so she'd have some help with the laundry.

He could simply ask Armen about the assassination, but Armen would deny it.

If he could just find something.

The locks were no problem. Vrezh had picked them a dozen times, enjoying the simple mechanical challenge. As a teenager, he'd spent long afternoons alone with stacks of espionage magazines, learning to read the deltas and ridges of fingerprints, teaching himself to pick locks. If he were Australian, he might have become a spy.

Armen's desk held sheaves of ARF paperwork, the words *Armenian Revolutionary Federation* encircling the crossed quill, sword, shovel and flagpole. They'd attended ARF meetings together, until Armen stopped without explanation. What could have taken his brother away from something so central to himself?

Vrezh had his suspicions even then.

The trunk held Armen's box of medals, most for boxing, some for wrestling. In the bedroom the boys had shared in Egypt, their father would hang each of Armen's medals on the wall beside his bed. Car headlights would catch the reflective surfaces, the medals winking at Vrezh as he lay on the other side of the room. The wall above Vrezh's childhood bed was empty. In Year 12, he received a gold medal in the science fair. His father never suggested hanging it. Vrezh left the medal dangling from his doorknob, where it clattered whenever he opened the door. After a week, he moved the medal to his sock drawer.

From outside came the rumble of an oversized engine, the metallic slam of a door. Vrezh's heart stopped – if Armen caught him, who knew what he'd do. Flip out, smash something. Maybe never speak to Vrezh again.

Vrezh peered through the narrow slat of window exposed under the blind. Could Armen be stopping in for lunch already?

The Rug King delivery van wasn't in their driveway. It wasn't sitting just past the trimmed hedgerow that divided their garden from Whiting Street. Vrezh scanned the row of tidy houses, the Fords and Commodores lined up along the kerb, but the large white van with its side-panel logo, a gold crown atop a stack of rolled carpets, wasn't there.

Maybe he was hearing things.

Underneath the medals was a folded tricolour Armenian flag. Picking it up, Vrezh's mind went to the marches. One of the first times he'd paid real attention to flags. Cairo, 1965.

He was six, stepping inside the club's gated courtyard, where torches illuminated a cluster of boys in haphazard lines loosely arranged from oldest to youngest. They marched round the courtyard, most dragging flags, some hoisting the burning torches.

Armen hustled Vrezh into the midst of the marching boys. Fathers and grandfathers stood to the side, arms crossed, expressions heavy, shouting an occasional command. It was a familiar place, but the torch smoke and the hardened faces, even among boys his age, made the place feel foreign.

He tried to slip his hand into Armen's.

His brother slapped his hand away. *What's wrong with you?* Armen wore his boxing ring face: focused eyes, tense jaw, tight lips. He shoved the corner of a blood red flag into Vrezh's chest. Grabbing it, Vrezh flicked his wrist and the flag twitched, its single white star and crescent moon not so different from the ones visible overhead.

They marched in circles, dragging the flags over the courtyard bricks. The jerking shadows cast by the torchlight reached out for him. His father and grandfather leant against the concrete wall, their thin Egyptian cigarettes trailing smoke. If Vrezh dropped the flag and ran to them, if he said he wanted to go home, they would call him a coward. His eyes welled. He sunk two teeth into his lower lip.

The column swung right and Armen popped into view, marching ahead, torch hoisted in one hand, flag trailing from the other. Chest puffed out like a warrior's. Vrezh tried to mimic his movements. The rhythm of the march came into his legs and his knees lifted higher.

At the following year's march, Vrezh stomped the blood-red flags with enthusiasm. Now the march fitted like a puzzle piece into his grandmother's stories. Across the courtyard, Vrezh sought his grandfather's eyes. The older boys poured kerosene on the heap of Turkish flags, and the crowd sang memorials to bloodied soldiers sacrificing themselves for their homeland as the *whoosh* of the flame caught, their eyes stinging with the foul smoke. Even then, Vrezh sensed these rituals were bound up in the meaning of his name – *revenge*.

Shaking his head to clear the rush of memories, Vrezh set aside the flag and emptied the rest of the wooden trunk. He pressed two fingers into the corner to reveal its false bottom. His brother often hid money there – surprising amounts, once over a thousand dollars – and sometimes photographs and timetables.

Vrezh reached into the dim space. Empty.

He stood in the middle of the room, traces of stale cigarette smoke and Ice cologne in his nostrils.

Pulling all the heavy wooden drawers from the desk, Vrezh set them on the rug, the same traditional Armenian rug that had been in their shared bedroom in Egypt.

Footsteps in the hall hit Vrezh like a lightning bolt to the chest and he jumped to his feet. Drawers were spread across half the room. He'd never get them back in place.

Vrezh flung himself toward the door, pressing his face into the carpeting to glimpse through the narrow crack. If Armen was heading for him, the door would smash his face.

Dainty feet in flesh-tone tights turned, headed into the adjacent bedroom. Just his mother. He sighed silent relief.

He remained motionless until she retreated to the kitchen, then replaced the drawers in slow motion. As an afterthought, he ran his hand along the wooden seams of the desk's interior – and that's where he found what he needed.

*

Soghomon Tehlirian. A teenager in rags in the desert, witness to the soldiers murdering his mother, raping his sister, splitting his brother's head open with an axe.

Tehlirian coming to consciousness in a pile of corpses. A sort of good fortune, that the future Armenian hero wasn't thrown into a well or some rocky chasm to be crushed by the bodies of others.

Tehlirian, a tall, reedy adult, his face sketched in simple lines, a billboard forehead. On the surface, he was a sombre foreigner in Berlin to study mechanical engineering. In fact, Tehlirian had come to stalk Mehmet Talaat.

Of all the men who planned the great crime against the Armenians during the First World War, there was Mehmet Talaat, Minister of Interior Affairs. The title belied his power.

When the Turks lost the war, the German government helped these men escape. Smug Talaat, fat like a walrus, climbed abroad a submarine in Bolis – what the world calls Istanbul – and stole away to Berlin.

Mehmet Talaat, convicted war criminal, tried in absentia, sentenced to death, yet living in Berlin under an assumed name.

Talaat and Tehlirian on Hardenbergstrasse. This was Tehlirian's moment. His long, steady stride, the angle of his brown fedora, the way he concealed his pistol. Sometimes it rested at the small of his back, other times it was tucked into a holster hidden by his pressed coat.

And now, here came Tehlirian, crossing the bitumen toward Talaat, passing him so he could confirm every detail of that walrus face, naked now without its trademark moustache. Tehlirian turning, drawing the pistol.

Firing a single shot.

Vrezh started awake. The lounge room, sharp December sun in the windows, his grandfather snoring in his armchair, wrapped in blankets despite the muggy air. He stood up, confused – had he seen Armen since the assassination? No, no, he'd been waiting for him to turn up for lunch.

The dream's sensations lingered. More often he dreamt of his great-grandfather in the moonlit night, hung from thick rope, vacant eyes open, his face blurring into Vrezh's own father's. After that first telling in their Cairo kitchen, Vrezh had heard Arshag's story many more times. Always from Seda. He'd imagined the experience so often, the details seemed to feel like Vrezh's own memories. He could feel the broiling sun, the sharp rocks under his bare feet. He could smell the blood of the little boy who would have been his great uncle.

Tehlirian in Berlin, 1921. *That* was the antidote. Decades before Vrezh was born. Yet lingering on the moment Tehlirian took aim – when victim became avenger – was like the drip of a morphine IV.

Other events took place before Vrezh was born: the return of Talaat's remains to Istanbul, sent by the Nazis, special delivery. Talaat's ceremonial burial at Istanbul's Monument of Liberty. The naming of Turkish streets in Talaat's honour, and an elementary school.

How the Turks had gotten away with it for so long, Vrezh couldn't understand. But that would all change. He patted his pocket, where the scrap of paper retrieved from inside his brother's desk waited.

*

Vrezh quickstepped the three blocks to Uncle Dikran's carpet store, shoulders hunched, thumbs squeezed inside fists.

Armen had been working for Uncle Dikran since they first arrived in Sydney, back when Dikran sold rugs from his lounge room and cleaned carpets in his garage. Dikran, the self-decreed Rug King, often told Armen to 'be more entrepreneurial, think bigger.' But maybe Armen would clean carpets all his life.

The shopfront bell jangled as Vrezh pushed through the glass door.

'Is Armen here?'

Dikran shrugged, ran a hand over his bald head. 'Should arrive any time. You want to help in back?'

Vrezh had spent many afternoons in the cleaning room, a high-ceilinged, fluorescent-lit concrete space, garage-like. The routine was familiar. He diluted the rug cleaning powder, its astringent smell stinging his sinuses. He set the cleaning machine at the correct height for the thickness of the pile, and pushed it over each rug with slow steps.

Was Armen the shooter? When Vrezh asked the question, it was himself he pictured climbing off the Honda's pillion seat, walking toward the car, drawing the gun, aiming through the windscreen. He was surrounded by two dozen hanging rugs in Uncle Dikran's cleaning warehouse, but he felt himself on the street in Vaucluse, Sydney's early morning sun heating his motorcycling leather, his arm raised, fingers tight around the gun handle.

Using the pulley, he hung each freshly clean rug over wooden beams, catching their underbellies on the beams' exposed nails and hoisting them toward the ceiling.

The Rug King delivery van arrived as the day's heat peaked. The metal door creaked upwards, and the van rolled into the far side of the cleaning room. Armen climbed out, t-shirt sleeves bunched over his shoulders. He wore aviators, his eyes mirrored. Sweat streaked his forehead. Was he nervous, thinking about the police closing in? He couldn't help but sweat though – the van had no air conditioning.

The police had found the Honda 500 used in the assassination, abandoned in Bondi. A $100,000 reward and still no suspects. The police theorised that the assassins had left the country, that they'd been flown in for the job. A suggestion to cover up their ineptitude, Vrezh guessed. Unless they were paid off. The Australian police were surprisingly corrupt.

'Hey,' Armen called, pointing this thumb over his shoulder, toward the van full of tightly rolled rugs. He strode up to the side door of Dikran's office.

Vrezh hesitated a moment too long, no words coming to him, and Armen was gone. His mouth felt dry. Cicadas buzzed like a headache.

The driver – or the shooter? A curious pride drove the question. And envy. His brother had followed in Tehlirian's footsteps. He was an Armenian hero. What did that make Vrezh? A nothing, all the worse because his own brother had left him out.

Armen reappeared in the doorway, eyes swinging from Vrezh to the rug-filled van.

'Get these outta here, what're you doing?'

Vrezh stood between Armen and the van, his voice lowered. 'I know about yesterday.'

Armen shoved past him.

'I've got more houses to hit. C'mon.'

Vrezh pulled the map from the back pocket of his jeans. It'd been caught in the desk's wooden seam, unintentionally, Vrezh assumed. A couple of folded squares torn from a larger map, Vaucluse and Dover Heights, a route traced in pen. Not the exact route yesterday's assassins had used, but it started from the consul's house. An early draft? How long had Armen been planning this? Who had he worked with?

And how could Vrezh join them?

Armen snatched the map fragment, his lighter under its corner. By the time Vrezh's limbs reacted, grabbing for the paper, it was already in flames. Armen dropped the last corner on the concrete floor and crushed it into ash under his shoe.

'You're supposed to be the smart one in the family.' His voice low, steel running through it.

'Tell me what you're planning.' Vrezh tried to match Armen's tone, but desperation lingered.

'There's nothing.' Grabbing a broom, Armen swept the traces of ash into the grated drain. Then he started hauling rugs, piling them along the wall.

Vrezh followed, close enough to see the textured ridges of the scar across Armen's left cheek, memento of a late night in Kings Cross. 'I want in!'

Armen leant in fast, his body tensed, fists tight. Then he turned and grabbed another rug, the sweat patch on the back of his shirt spreading.

Vrezh grabbed a rug too. Said nothing.

When the van was empty, Armen drove away.

*

By the time the family moved to Australia, Armen had only a few months of school left; he didn't bother with it. But Vrezh found himself in a classroom full of red-headed Rebeccas and sandy-haired Jasons. In their mouths, *Vrezh* became *Reg*. The pale, speckled Aussie kids teased him about the *dolma*, vine leaves stuffed with rice and lamb his mother packed for lunch, about his clumsiness on the rugby field. About his name.

At Armenian school in North Ryde, the kids looked like him, even though their families had moved from Iran and Israel, Lebanon and Turkey. And Egypt. They sang and studied history and read the great Armenian poets and ate *dolma*, all wishing they didn't have to spend their Saturdays in class.

In Year 7 at The Forest High School, Vrezh's class researched their family trees, crafting them on poster-paper, branches extending from their earliest known relatives. One of his classmates could trace ten generations. Others were descendants of Australia's first colonists.

Vrezh was keen to complete the assignment. But Seda, his grandmother, had been left at the gate of the British consulate in Moush, as a toddler. She didn't know her own name, let alone the names of her parents. A nun had called her Seda. And Arshag never spoke his parents' names. Seda had known them, but she was no longer alive to ask.

It was the same with his mother's family. Wiped from history.

Vrezh left most of his tree blank, without explanation. His teacher scolded him for his lack of effort.

His Year 9 class studied the Holocaust. As Vrezh was completing his homework at the dining room table one evening, his father saw the textbook open to photos of Bergen-Belsen. He hurled the book to the floor. 'Wasting your time on the attention-seeking Jews!'

Vrezh's Year 11 history teacher, Mrs Thomas, assigned individual presentations. Students would write a report on any twentieth-century historical figure of their choice. Vrezh chose Tehlirian without a thought to anyone else, even General Antarig.

He was finally ready to share Armenia's story. He'd accepted the poor grades on his family tree, on his Holocaust essay, feeling ashamed and confused. Now he wrote about the genocide and Mehmet Talaat and the war tribunals of 1919 that declared Talaat guilty in absentia. And how, two years later, Tehlirian assassinated Talaat in the street in Berlin with that one clean shot.

Vrezh imagined Talaat collapsing in the street with little fanfare, his horrible, earthshaking power gone before his head touched the pavement.

In that moment, Tehlirian gave himself up to the Germans. At the trial, the judge listened to Tehlirian's story.

About the deaths of his mother and sister and brother. Other witnesses came, German men. They spoke about the actions of their wartime ally.

The judge declared Soghomon Tehlirian not guilty. For Vrezh, this was proof that justice, if as rare as snow in Sydney, did exist. For his grandparents' families left unburied in the deserts east of Bolis, for all the Armenians like himself barred from their homeland, there was one shining moment of true justice.

Vrezh presented Tehlirian's story in Mrs Thomas's class. His peers were still mostly blondes and gingers, though a few mirrored his darker complexion. One of these olive-skinned students, he later learnt, was a Turk.

The following week, Vrezh was called to the principal's office.

*

Vrezh sucked in a shaky breath, then climbed into the Commodore's boot. It was 5 am. Curling into the awkward space, he checked his pockets one last time. Penlight, compass, strip of duct tape to rig the boot lock so he could let himself out.

He pulled the lid closed.

It'd been a month since the assassination, and Armen wasn't saying anything.

The first time Vrezh tried to follow Armen's burgundy '76 Commodore, he hung back too far and immediately lost him. Borrowing his father's Centura was tricky enough, not knowing when exactly he'd return, and the damned lemon yellow paint was too recognisable. Vrezh lost Armen a second time just outside Willoughby, and a third, not much further.

He wasn't enthused with this new plan. It felt like a high school caper, the sort of thing he might have done as a teen. If he'd had any friends to do it with.

Vrezh's calves were already cramping when he heard the scuffing of dress shoes on bitumen. Dress shoes – an Armenian trait. Any Australian would be wearing slapping thongs on a hot Saturday. Vrezh had debated with himself that morning and finally decided on trainers, unsure if he might need to make a quiet escape.

It must be Armen. Their father would never get up so early on a Saturday. Vrezh tensed, praying his brother didn't have a reason to open the boot.

The door creaked, the car shifted.

He fixed the penlight on the compass. It spun randomly. Vrezh wanted to slap himself. Of course the compass wouldn't work surrounded by the metal of the boot.

They were on a highway, judging by the consistent high speed. Vrezh checked his Timex again. And again. The car droned on the smooth surface. He'd assumed Armen was going somewhere in Sydney, but they must be outside the city by now. Maybe he had it all wrong. Maybe Armen had a secret girlfriend in Wollongong, some blonde who walked barefoot to the shops.

He tried to picture the landscape they might be passing. Fields. Cattle. Gum trees. He wondered what the land had looked like when there were only Aboriginals here, but the thought flitted away. Vrezh had never met an Aboriginal, wasn't much interested. Instead he daydreamt of the powerful, snowcapped mountains of Armenia. He longed to breathe the air of his homeland, to dig his hands into its earth. But even getting a tourist visa to the USSR was difficult.

Suddenly Vrezh's head slammed against the boot, shocking him awake. His mouth opened in a shout of pain but he caught himself, just. Gravel ricocheted beneath him and the ride became rough. He braced himself, straining. This must be a driveway.

But the bumping continued another forty minutes before the car slowed, stopped, the engine cut out.

The door opened and slammed shut, shoes crunched on gravel. Armen's footsteps receded, vanished. A currawong called. Then silence.

Vrezh waited. He'd been squeezed in the boot for almost five hours. His whole body ached.

Biting his lip, he released the duct tape from the lock and cracked the lid.

For a moment he was blind. Then, bush. A thick gnarl of gum trees, scrub, tan-coloured rocks. Nothing else.

Where was Armen? The car must be facing whatever building was out here – unless this was just a rendezvous point in the middle of nowhere.

If he got out, he might be able to peer under the car, figure out what to do.

Hearing nothing, Vrezh pushed the boot's lid up just wide enough for his shoulders. He tried to slither out, but his hamstring seized and he collapsed onto the sandy gravel. He gripped his thigh to quell the spasm.

Footsteps came fast toward him.

'Stay down!'

But adrenaline caused Vrezh to shoot up, palms at chest height, his heart seizing. He'd hardly processed the figure coming at him when he was struck across the face and landed abruptly on his back, skidding over rough stones.

'Fuck, it's my brother.'

Vrezh didn't recognise the first voice – older, booming, a strong Armenian accent. But the second, heavy with annoyance, was Armen's.

The stranger held a pistol pointed low, right at him.

'Get up, Vrezh. What the fuck?'

Vrezh didn't move. Pain spread across the left side of his face into his temple, his teeth.

'It's okay, Softie, it's just my idiot brother.'

Softie slid the gun away. 'So this is Vrezh Melokian.' Vrezh recognised the accent. *Gyumretsi* – from Armenia's north.

Standing, Vrezh could make out the wrinkles around Softie's eyes, the grey streaks in his hair. A man in his fifties maybe, but solid, his chest twice as wide as Vrezh's, his shoulders military square.

'A pleasure to finally meet you,' Softie said, extending his now-empty hand.

Sunlight shone through narrow, glowing windows in the corrugated tin shed, a space the size of a three-car garage, filled with scattered worktables, rusting farm equipment, half an ancient ute. A folded blanket and thin pillow sat at the head of a military surplus cot. Dust drifted.

'I understand you took it upon yourself to get here today, Vrezh.' Even when his words were casual, threat rumbled in Softie's voice. The gun – a Beretta, Vrezh thought, though he'd only ever seen pictures – was holstered at his hip. 'It must have been an uncomfortable journey. Your efforts show determination.'

Vrezh nodded his thanks. Blood trickled beneath a wadded up handkerchief pressed to his nose.

'Retrieve another glass for us, Armen.' Softie gestured to the bottle of Armenian cognac and two glasses arranged on one of the worktables.

Armen ground his jaw as he brought a grimy glass, wiping it with his shirt.

Softie settled onto a tall stool and poured the cognac. 'Sit, sit.'

Vrezh did as told. Armen remained standing, arms crossed, his hip against the ute's corroded cab.

'Has Armen described to you our efforts?' Softie kept his gaze on Armen, and didn't wait for Vrezh to answer. 'Armen and I are part of a brotherhood with a sacred duty. My father was part of General Antarig's orphan army. Despite our struggles much of our homeland remains in the blood-stained hands of the Turks.' Softie raised his shot. Armen and Vrezh followed. 'To a free and prosperous Armenia.'

As soon as the empty glasses were set on the table, Softie refilled them.

'I have insisted Armen bring you to meet me for several months, Vrezh. Every time I ask, he has excuses. I began to suspect I would have to find you myself. Now here you are. Like destiny.'

Softie's eyes bore through him like an x-ray.

'I'd have gladly come any time, sir.' He glanced at Armen, who glared.

'I have heard you are studying at Sydney University.'

'I started a PhD last year.'

'Tell me, Vrezh, have you heard about the shooting of Mr Ariyak that occurred in December?'

Vrezh nodded, wondering what kind of test this was.

'And what was your opinion?' Two gold teeth glinted between Softie's lips.

Vrezh pushed his glasses up with his index finger and wiggled on the stool, trying to sit a little taller.

'It lived up to Tehlirian's example. Punishing those responsible for the genocide and its denial. It was just, and brought attention to our cause. I was – I was very impressed.'

Softie raised an eyebrow. Then he locked eyes with Armen and nodded as if in slow motion before pouring three more shots.

'Your intelligence is obvious, Vrezh. Many people have told me this.'

Vrezh gave a small nod, but privately felt the glow of recognition.

Softie lifted his glass again. 'To your father's health and the freedom of our beloved homeland.'

It was that easy. Vrezh strode out of the shed, raising his smiling face toward the blue sky. He turned to Armen, for a moment thinking his brother might offer to shake his hand, welcome him to their splinter of the Justice Commandos.

Armen slammed the car door. He gripped the steering wheel like he might tear it from the console.

Vrezh crossed his arms, keeping his eyes on the barren landscape rushing past. Armen lit one Marlboro after another, the smoke rushing out the open window.

They were on the highway by the time Vrezh broke. He smacked his fists to his thighs.

'You dick! Softie wanted to meet me. You never told me!'

'I'm about two seconds from flinging your door open and kicking you out of this damn car! You have no idea what you've gotten into.'

'Fine, I'm so stupid – tell me.'

Armen shook his head. 'You know why he's called Softie?' He flicked ash onto the mound spilling out of the Commodore's tray. 'A joke. He was in the Battle of Berlin in '45, eighteen years old. Ran out of ammo, killed a Nazi with half of a brick. Got out of the USSR, ended up in Beirut. He's got ties to the PLO. You don't fuck around with the PLO.'

'So what's his real name?'

'Listen to me! You gotta have balls to work with someone like Softie. This isn't for chess-playing lightweights!'

Vrezh's fists came up in frustration. 'You think you're the only person in the family who can be a hero!'

Armen responded with reflexive defense, his left fist raised, then opened to slap the back of Vrezh's head, their father's trademark move.

Vrezh batted Armen's hand away, shouting. Armen shouted back, leaning into Vrezh's face as the car veered into the oncoming lane, and only at the last possible second did the scream of a horn and the dodging manoeuvre of the ute driver shock Armen's focus back to the highway. He righted the Commodore with both hands on the wheel and the rage of every lost boxing match in his eyes.

'Try not to get us killed,' Vrezh muttered.

*

The Forest High School principal wore a black vest with a wide white strip over his white dress shirt. He tented his hands when he spoke. On the corner of his desk sat a lamp and some kind of droopy pot plant, with curved leaves trailing down the side of the desk, but this didn't make the place any more comfortable to Vrezh. Through the closed window, past the closed blinds, he could hear his classmates shouting, a game of rugby gearing up. The office smelt like liniment, an old man smell.

'The problem, Reg, is that history isn't so – straightforward, you understand.' In the pause he ran his tongue over his top front teeth, his upper lip bulging with the movement. Vrezh was resigned to the mispronunciation of his name, but the principal's tongue disgusted him. 'Mrs Thomas completed an Honours degree in history, wrote her thesis on

Renaissance influences in Tudor England, in fact. She knows how contentious various – narratives can be.'

He gestured to his left, where Mrs Thomas sat with her arms tight against her chest, nodding.

'In light of your, let's say, *glorification* of an assassin, which your classmate Kerem – and his *parents* – found personally offensive, his parents have asked that you be suspended and removed from Mrs Thomas's class.'

Across the wide desk, Vrezh sat, shoulders hunched, hands shoved under his thighs. Since arriving in Australia, his relationship with teachers had been strained. Now this, his first time in the principal's office. And that baby Kerem, crying to his parents.

'Do you have anything to say to that, Reg?' The tongue again.

Vrezh shrugged, eyes on the floor.

'Well. We feel it's an unnecessary step – at this stage. However, we've informed Kerem's parents that you have failed this assignment – which you have – and you'll be required to stay late for the next fortnight to complete a make-up assignment. An essay on Simpson and his donkey.'

'A true Aussie hero,' Mrs Thomas said.

'Which you'll read at the Anzac Day assembly on 24 April.'

Vrezh's fingernails dug into his palms.

*

The shed's metal siding was weathered, and cracks snaked across the concrete floor. The amount of grime and rusted machinery inside suggested it had sat for a long time. Longer than Softie seemed to have been in the country, Vrezh suspected. The roof came to a central point, with metal support beams running along it, giving the place the feel of a factory. A pair of worn work boots hung over one of the beams, knotted at the laces, an inch of dust on them. Cobwebs everywhere. Toolboxes and metal crates filled each corner. The tall, narrow windows let a good amount of light in, casting a pattern of dark and light patches.

Softie seemed to be living in a corner of the shed, at least some of the time. Beside the sink was a shelf with canned stew, the labels bright, the tops free of dust. The cot, with its pillow and single blanket, often looked freshly slept in when Vrezh and Armen arrived. There was a stack of clothes too, loosely folded, nothing like the perfect right-angled stacks Vrezh's mother tucked into the family's dresser drawers. The place smelt of grease, oil and the fake lemon of cleaning spray.

Armen had supplied the cleaning spray, Vrezh was sure. One of the first things he did after the long drive each week was to clear the large central table, spray it down and wipe it clean. Then he replaced the table's contents, setting each item square with the table's edge. Rolled maps, notebooks filled with blocky Armenian writing and the occasional English interjection, pens, pencils, phone books for Sydney and Canberra, a compass, odds and ends. He never asked Vrezh for help with this, just stepped around him if he hung out near the table during the ritual.

After the obligatory round of shots one afternoon, Softie turned to Armen.

'You would be advised to check the oil levels of your vehicle at this time.' Each word heavy.

This must be important. *Finally.*

It'd been two months, and Vrezh was getting antsy. Armen drove him out to the shearing shed about once a fortnight, the same Charles Aznavour cassette playing there and back.

Gathered around the central work table, the trio discussed the little evidence the police had on the Vaucluse shooting. The reward for information was now $250,000.

It made sense, lying low after Vaucluse – but why had Softie wanted to meet him if they weren't doing anything?

They discussed the Turkish officials in Australia, made note of any mention of them in the news. They analysed the news from Paris, where the Armenian Secret Army for the Liberation of Armenia, the sister organisation to the Justice Commandos, had assassinated two Turkish government officials.

But Softie said nothing about plans to come. Why weren't they discussing the next shooting?

Armen headed outside, narrowed eyes fixed on his brother. He walked past the car and up the road, Marlboro at his lips.

Softie leant toward him, his voice low. 'Vrezh. You understand that by coming here, you're implicated in what this country's government views as criminal activity. This is a fact.'

Vrezh nodded. *This was the moment.* Softie was finally going to reveal their next target, and Vrezh's role. Was this how Tehlirian felt when he was invited to join Operation Nemesis, when he learnt he would be tracking down Talaat?

'And you understand there is enough evidence against your brother to put him in prison for many years.'

Vrezh felt his cheek twitch, hoped it wasn't visible. He nodded again.

'Your grandparents suffered at the hands of the Turks as my parents did, as their families did. Are you prepared to become a soldier for our sacred cause?'

The air felt electric. Vrezh gave another sharp nod.

'Excellent.' Softie leant back, crossed his arms. 'Tell me what you know about ammonium nitrate.'

Vrezh blinked, thinking he'd misheard. The question floated between the two men for a moment, until the full meaning hit Vrezh like a bucket of ice water.

'I – uh, well, I haven't had much, uh, experience with ammonium. Actually, um, none. I know more about rifles and – '

Softie raised one meaty hand.

'Let me rephrase. I require you to be an expert on ammonium nitrate. Specifically in relation to detonation and timing equipment. Blast radius. Shrapnel. Alternatives and their advantages. Report back next week.'

The concrete floor turned to jelly beneath Vrezh. Despite the autumn chill, his glasses slid along the sweat of his nose.

All this time, he'd assumed they would plan another shooting.

*

The two hundred students of The Forest High School slumped in their auditorium chairs, few bothering to look at Vrezh. Still, his tongue had become a dead slug. He gripped the edges of the wooden podium.

'Tomorrow is April 25,' Vrezh began.

The principal and Mrs Thomas didn't realise it, but they'd given him an opportunity.

He inched closer to the microphone.

Yesterday Mrs Thomas had made him read his Anzac speech aloud twice before letting him go home. Now he began with the same lines.

'It's an important day in Australia, known as Anzac Day.'

The principal sat a metre away from him on the stage.

'But today is April 24 and it's also an important day. Today commemorates fifty-six years since the Armenian genocide, when the Ottoman Empire killed one million Armenians.'

He'd laboured over the secret version of his speech, reading every Anzac history book in the library. That bastard Charles Bean, the great Australian war historian, hadn't even mentioned the genocide.

'Hours before the Anzac troops landed at Gallipoli, Turkish authorities arrested more than 200 Armenian reli-gious and cultural leaders, as well as teachers. They were taken away to be tortured and killed.'

The principal was pushing himself to his feet now. Mrs Thomas was heading up the stage steps, straight for Vrezh.

The students snapped out of their stupor, four hundred eyeballs locking onto him.

It was Alan Moorehead's *Gallipoli* that came through for Vrezh, with three whole pages about the genocide.

Adrenaline replaced Vrezh's nerves. If they could hear this part, they'd understand. Moorehead's words ran together.

'The government's system "was to goad the Armenians to the point where they attempted to resist. At first their goods were requisitioned, then the women were molested, and finally the shooting began." An Australian –'

The principal grabbed Vrezh's arm, tugging at him. The auditorium swayed around him, but he strained forward. If he could just finish, if they'd just let him talk. He lunged for the microphone just as Mrs Thomas yanked it away.

'Liar!' A voice from the crowd. '*He's lying!*'

Kerem.

'An Australian wrote that,' Vrezh yelled, trying to twist out of the principal's grasp. 'An Australian wrote that!'

The principal and another teacher had his upper arms and were pulling him away. He kicked out a leg, trying to hook the edge of the podium. He struck its edge, and the bulky wooden thing teetered, then crashed to the stage, catching Mrs Thomas on the foot.

The typed pages of Vrezh's speech scattered like leaves. Students were on their feet now, cat-calling, enjoying the commotion, while teachers shouted at them to sit down. The red-faced principal, stubby fingers clamped to Vrezh's bicep, pulled him off the stage.

Vrezh waited in the principal's office alone for an hour, his adrenaline gone. When the principal came through the door, he jumped to his feet, thrusting a copy of his speech from his jacket pocket into the principal's hands. If he would just read what Vrezh had written, he'd understand. The truth was there, even in the Australian history books. You just had to look for it.

'What is this?' The principal glanced at the pages, then balled them up and dropped them in the bin. 'Mrs Thomas is in hospital for x-rays. They suspect at least two cracked bones in her foot. She'll be on crutches for weeks.'

Vrezh's cheeks burned.

Part of his punishment was apologising to Kerem and his parents, his knees shaking with humiliation as he stood in front of them in the principal's cramped office later that week.

'What did you do to get expelled?' his father bellowed when the phone call came, that one forehead vein pulsing.

His mother held a hand over her heart. 'Disruptive conduct, Vrezh, what does it mean?'

'Got in a fight,' Vrezh muttered. Shame burned in his chest. He couldn't bear to admit how he'd failed them.

Later Vrezh learnt that Kerem's father worked at the Turkish Consulate.

*

For days Vrezh dragged himself around the house, his mind churning over the possibility of a bomb. He'd abandoned his PhD work, pleaded illness to his supervisor.

'Vrezh, *jan*, are you alright?' his mother asked, the *lahma-joon* she'd prepared uneaten on his plate.

'Fine, *mayrig*.' He couldn't meet her eyes.

Alone in his room, he reread his stack of clippings about ASALA and Justice Commando attacks, kept in his own desk's secret compartment. Hunched over the articles in the midnight quiet, he dug his toes into the thick pile of the rug beneath him, feeling as though he'd swallowed acid.

There'd been car bombings in Athens, all unsuccessful. A few bombs at Turkish Airlines offices, with bystanders injured.

He'd always imagined Tehlirian having absolute conviction in his actions. Now Vrezh wondered if Tehlirian had questioned himself as he raised his gun on the street. He would have only known Talaat's face from the grainy black-and-whites of the era. Tehlirian had killed the right man – but how had he known at the moment he'd drawn the pistol? Did the risk of a stray bullet hitting one of the German civilians on Hardenbergstrasse cross his mind?

At the same desk where he'd re-written his Anzac Day speech a decade earlier, Vrezh dropped his head into his hands. Could he actually set a bomb, watch it go off? Maybe if it were a car bomb, if they knew the car's owner would be alone, if they had a remote detonator, could be precise …

It would be simpler once Vrezh knew Softie's plan.

On their next trip to the shearing shed, under black churning clouds that broke into pounding rain, he briefed Softie on his ammonium nitrate research, expecting a discussion about possible tactics.

There was no discussion. Softie gave Vrezh specifications and told him to get to work.

'We have a deadline. I am confident you understand the necessity of meeting it.' Softie's voice was low and dark.

Vrezh and Armen made the trip to the shearing shed most weekends, usually Saturdays. Softie requested updates on the cold details of compounds and blast radius, and Vrezh's progress. A tangle of wires, timing components, and handfuls of nails and ball bearings covered Vrezh's worktable. Vrezh tried to ignore the shrapnel.

Armen said nothing.

At home, Vrezh noted Armen's long absence more than once. He suspected his brother was with Softie, discussing the plan's full scope. In private.

It was as though Vrezh was outside a locked room, his face pressed to the keyhole, a sliver of activity all that was visible.

One Saturday the brothers arrived to find a rubbish truck parked beside the shearing shed. A hint of rot lingered around the truck.

'So the truck's part of things, Softie?' Vrezh asked, cups of coffee steaming on the table.

Armen glared at him. Softie's moustache curled at one side, lifted by a half-smile.

'A curious nature is the mark of a scientific mind, Vrezh *jan*.'

When Softie finished his coffee, he walked outside, to the rudimentary shooting range alongside the shed, and started picking off the Coke cans in the distance. The gunshots rang in Vrezh's ears.

*

The cold gripped most of the house, but Vrezh's mother ran the oil heater in Arshag's mothballed bedroom. She and Vrezh took turns passing the night there, to wake the old man before his nightmares overtook him. The lounge room sofa was too far away, his mother insisted. She feared a heart attack.

One night, the creak of the back door snapped Vrezh from his half-slumber in the worn armchair. It was 1 am. Arshag's eyes were closed, his face relaxed.

Leaving the bedroom door slivered open, Vrezh stepped into the kitchen. The stove light cast a dim glow.

'How's Softie?'

Armen had a mouthful of *dolma*, taken cold from the fridge. He slid the container across the table, toward Vrezh. The *dolma* were slick with olive oil.

Vrezh reached for a chair, then turned and began to pace the linoleum. Four steps forward, four steps back.

'Look, Armen. Just – is Softie going to tell me what the plan is?'

Armen took another bite, chewed. The weak light from the stove left half his face in shadow.

'I thought…' Vrezh felt his ribs tighten. 'Okay, look, I assumed it was like, well, Vaucluse. We pick a target and we kill that person as – as justice.' He stopped, crossed his arms tight, squeezing them against his chest. 'This thing Softie's having me build … it's not going to be one or two people.'

But Armen must already know that.

Didn't he realise what it meant?

Armen huffed, shook his head once. He matched Vrezh's whisper and it came out as a hiss. 'What the hell did you think was going to happen when you got in the boot of my car? You'd just stroll in, have a look around, see if things were to your liking? Softie and me didn't need you sticking your ugly nose in.'

The rubbish truck was part of the plan. Vrezh had overheard Softie and Armen talking about it. Someone would drive it to the chosen destination. Park. Climb out. Start to walk away.

'I need to know where this thing is going off.'

Vrezh had a suspicion. Turkey's Minister of Foreign Affairs, İlter Türkmen, would be in Canberra on June 20. *The Australian* had an article about it.

June 20. Three weeks from now.

Armen chewed, swallowed. Took another *dolma* with his fingertips as he leant back, the kitchen chair creaking under his weight. 'You're clever, Vrezh.'

'So it's the embassy. That's why we're out near Canberra.'

Armen thrust his chin out.

'But what if there's other people?' This was the key question, *this, now, ask it ask it ask it.* 'When will it go off? In the daytime?'

'They're Turks, *Vrezh.*' Angry, derisive. 'Why don't you live up to your name?'

'Other people go to embassies! Australian people – hell, what if there's Bolsahay there, getting some paperwork or something?' Bolsahay, the thousands of Armenians who still lived in Istanbul. Turkish citizens.

Why doesn't that worry you?

Armen pulled out a cigarette, looked at Vrezh above the lighter's flame. The refrigerator's rumbling cut out abruptly, leaving a hollow silence. Vrezh listened for any sound from Arshag's room.

His mind raced through what fragments of the plan he knew. The bomb would be in the rubbish truck. Rubbish trucks only came around in the daytime. When the embassy was likely to be full of people.

But maybe there was something Vrezh had missed.

'Just tell me when you're going to set it off.'

Armen threw his head back. 'What *difference* does it make? You've gotta finish it either way. And you've gotta be more careful around Softie.' He stabbed a finger toward Vrezh. 'Yes or no, nothing else. You've been asking too many damn questions.'

'We can't kill a bunch of Australians! That makes us – '

'We need to make a *statement*. Besides, you think Softie's going to let you take a pass?'

Vrezh squeezed the heels of his hands against his temples. How quickly could Softie have Armen arrested for the Vaucluse assassination? Would he wait around to collect the $250,000 reward – or just hand over the evidence and disappear back to Beirut? Vrezh pictured his mother collapsing at the news of Armen's conviction. Her eldest son.

'Just finish it.' Smoke hung above Armen's head. 'I'll make sure you don't have to do anything else.'

Vrezh stared at his hands. 'Are you setting it off?'

Armen shook his head. 'Too many questions.'

*

The Armenian Cultural Centre in Willoughby had the chill of a freezer. Three-dozen men sat in their overcoats, scarves wrapped tight, their hands gripping lukewarm cups of gritty coffee.

Two of the Revolutionary Federation directors were debating the executive director about a point from last meeting's minutes, a budget item incorrectly allocated. The three men spoke over each other.

Vrezh couldn't focus. Across the hall, the winning image of that year's community art exhibition was directly in his line of sight. An oil work, *Armenians hanging in the streets of Anatolia*, their heads at unnatural angles, bodies limp. Their faces were his father's face.

He could feel each of his neck muscles, taut like the ropes in the painting. His scarf was choking him. He removed it with exaggerated slowness, certain the action would betray his guilt. The guilt of not being utterly committed – of not being his brother.

Just finish it.

Vrezh's fought his urge to run from the hall.

He couldn't go through with it. Even if someone else placed the bomb, if someone else detonated it – he was building the thing. He'd be responsible for any innocent people. This wasn't justice.

Why don't you live up to your name?

It was as if Armen had sliced through the flesh of his chest, peeling it away to reveal a heart that was Armenian, but not sufficiently so.

His mind raced in a loop. Armen in the dim kitchen light – *just finish it*. His high school principal taking the Turks' side, erasing the crimes against his homeland, his family. A lake of blood from the little boy who would never grow up to be his great uncle.

It had all been simple when he was young. Armen was his role model for bravery, Tehlirian his hero.

Now Vrezh had an opportunity to punish a denialist – a Turkish *minister*.

And he couldn't do it.

The man beside him interrupted loudly, something about the date of an upcoming fundraiser.

For the first time, Vrezh wondered if the Turks had meetings like this when they planned the genocide. If walrus-faced Talaat and the members of the Committee of Union and Progress drank bad coffee and discussed budget items while they finalised details for the release of violent prison convicts on the condition they murdered Armenians.

Just finish it.

If he sat with Softie and Armen making plans that resulted in the deaths of innocent people, was he any different?

Vrezh walked home along dark streets, twice making wrong turns. Possums scuttled along branches overhead, screeching.

Justice was worth sacrificing yourself for. But Softie's plan – if Vrezh understood it – wasn't justice.

What were his options? He could go to the police, turn Softie in. He would, even if it meant he'd go to prison as well – but he couldn't risk the police discovering Armen's involvement.

He could walk away and sit at home, waiting for Softie to make good on his threats. Or for Armen to blow himself up tinkering with the half-built bomb.

There was one other thing he could do. But only if he knew without doubt what Softie had planned. He turned it over in his mind as he headed up the drive at 29 Whiting Street, past the hedgerow, onto his front step.

The front door's bolt thudded with the finality of a gavel.

Vrezh found his mother in the armchair next to Arshag's bed, a book of Charent's poems open in her lap, her eyes closed. Her chestnut curls, so tight in the morning, hung limp now, the patch above her right temple flattened where she tended to clamp a hand to her head in worry. He imagined the tears on her cheeks when she visited her sons in prison.

Whatever he did, he had to protect Armen, if only for his mother's sake.

'Mama, go to bed,' Vrezh whispered, his hand light on her shoulder. 'I will stay with *papik*.'

'Oh, Vrezh, he's been so upset tonight. Twice already I've coaxed him back to sleep.'

The armchair was still warm when he settled into it.

Hours later, Vrezh had a plan. It went against every-thing he'd been raised to believe. But it soothed that acidic gnawing he'd felt since the moment Softie had asked him to build a bomb.

Now, if he could just make it work.

*

Throughout the Saturday morning drive, the Aznavour cassette playing in the Commodore, Vrezh clenched and unclenched his hands. He silently practised the spiel he'd prepared.

At the shearing shed, Softie stood in front of the shed's narrow window, blocking the low-slanting sun like a solar eclipse. Vrezh couldn't make out the details of his face, but he could see the knife, the tip of which Softie was running under his fingernails.

'Describe to me your progress, Vrezh.'

Vrezh spread his hands wide over his workbench, the mess of wires and tools, the crude metal box he'd fashioned.

'Slow, Softie. The timing mechanism is – well, it's quite technical. I'm working with heat filament wire but it's not as reliable as I'd hoped. Is there – do we have other options? Or …' He trailed off.

These days, Vrezh worked through as many Marlboros as Armen. He had one lit now, the trail of smoke wavering, betraying his unsteady hand.

'I have made clear my instructions. True soldiers do not question their commander's intentions.'

'I'm pretty confident about the chemistry, but the timing mechanism is an issue for an electrician – or, I don't know, a watchmaker. Here.'

Vrezh picked up a metal box with wires spilling out of its core.

'I'm sure I can get it working, but it'll take some time to calibrate the terminals.' He monitored Softie's face to gauge how much of the technical explanation he understood. Not much, it seemed. Maybe his special forces training had focused on other areas. Or maybe 'special forces' was an exaggeration.

'This delay is no longer acceptable.' Softie didn't need to raise his voice. He pointed the knife toward Vrezh. 'You will provide me with a working model within the fortnight.'

Vrezh's recent purchase stayed concealed in his jacket pocket. It was second-hand, found through a classified ad in one of his military espionage magazines. Cash only, the seller had insisted.

He waited until Softie and Armen were outside, the first shots echoing from the firing range. Then he pulled out the recording device.

*

Standing in the kitchen at 5 am, Vrezh leant over the blank notepad, pen in hand. But if this was goodbye, he couldn't figure out how to say it. He couldn't even work out what to say to his father about the car. And the note might tip off Armen.

Armen would be tipped off pretty soon regardless – in the driveway, Vrezh popped the Commodore's bonnet and cut the spark plug wires.

As he pulled onto Whiting Street in his father's yellow Centura, he slowed, taking one last look at the house where he'd lived since primary school.

The speedometer stayed steady, just under the limit. Checking the clock, he stopped at a service station on the Hume Highway near Mittagong. He ordered a coffee and settled at a plastic table, watching the traffic pass.

Two days from now, the Turkish foreign minister would arrive in Canberra. In a way, Vrezh was sparing the man's life. The thought made him grimace. From one perspective, he was a traitor. But what else could he do? He'd analysed his options a thousand times, and he always came to the same conclusion. He would create his own justice, even if it was horrible.

The recording device had worked better than he'd hoped. He'd left it for a week, inside a mess of equipment he was sure Softie wouldn't bother to touch. Two days ago, he'd brought it home, listening late into the night while his family slept.

Sound activated above 50 decibels, the tiny device had captured a couple of hours of sporadic conversation. Somehow Softie had gotten copies of the embassy's blueprints, Vrezh learnt. The rubbish truck, packed with ammonium nitrate, would arrive at 11am – not long after the minister himself.

The bomb's timing mechanism was supposed to allow Armen just enough time to walk away.

Though faint and tinny, the recorded voices were audible.

'Half the building, at least.'

There it was: Softie's true face, cleansing Vrezh of any doubt.

'The only loose end is your brother.'

'I told you he wasn't cut out for this. Always overthinking everything. Makes him squeamish.'

'That he has proved to be a disappointment is immaterial. Whether he knows how to keep quiet, however —'

Hearing the threatening undertone channelled through headphones straight into his ear, Vrezh's heart seized.

'I'll make sure he does.'

The service station coffee was cold. Vrezh threw it out.

The turnoff to the shearing shed was unmarked, the route a zigzagging mess, but Vrezh had every turn memorised. Here were the two ghost gums, close at the base of their trunks, but wider apart the higher they went, a lonely V on the horizon. The gravel drive crested a barren hill and then dropped down toward the scraggle of gums and bush that mostly obscured the shearing shed.

Vrezh's knees threatened to buckle as he stepped out of the car. He slammed the door, overcompensating.

Softie came to the doorway, the collar of his black military jacket folded to avoid the shaving cream that covered half his face. A straight razor hung in his hand. His pistol sat snug in his hip holster.

'Vrezh *jan. Barev.*' A long slow pause as Vrezh's feet crunched over the gravel. 'You are on your own this morning.'

Vrezh forced himself to look Softie in the eyes as they shook hands in the doorway, their typical greeting. He tried to remember if Softie always squeezed that hard.

'Armen has the flu or something. Can't even stand up.' The words came out stiff. 'He said I could help get the truck loaded.'

Normally he and Armen sat with Softie over a coffee and a few shots of cognac. Softie asked about their parents. They discussed the latest ASALA attacks in Madrid or Beirut.

Today Vrezh crossed straight to his workbench, feeling as though Softie could see through him.

From here his plan became less certain.

The best-case scenario involved Vrezh getting back into the Centura and driving away. That was the version he'd concentrated on. But to do that, things had to look natural. He couldn't turn from his workbench and announce he was heading out after five minutes.

Water splashed in the basin.

'You are putting on the coffee, Vrezh?'

'One minute, I need to check something…'

Among the scattered mess, Vrezh twisted four wires together. It was a delicate task, the entirety of his plan. He focused his full attention on it, ensuring the bomb – adjusted to his own specifications – would do its job.

Suddenly Softie rushed toward him, his pistol trained on Vrezh.

'Step back! Now!'

Vrezh took two long, quick strides away from the table. He raised his hands, palms out, like he was in some stupid movie.

A rush of calm spread through his chest, like menthol. There were no more decisions to make. If he could run, he would. If not – well.

'It is very convenient of you to arrive here alone, Vrezh.'

There was no light on the bomb to indicate it was working. It was rudimentary, but also precise. Vrezh focused on sliding his foot backwards and bracing, keeping his eyes on Softie, who had positioned himself in front of the worktable.

'I was mistaken to think you could be relied on.' Softie centred the Beretta on Vrezh. 'But I never make the same mistake tw–'

Vrezh pivoted and leaped, feeling the momentary resistance of the window glass against his shoulder before its sudden release, a heartbeat before the silent blast of heat.

The shed lit up like a thousand terrible suns.

*

A stout nurse hovered over Vrezh, adjusting an IV.

'Reg, you are one lucky man.' Her strong Aussie accent, foreign and familiar. 'If your brother hadn't gotten you here so fast, you might have lost more than just your arm. He's a real hero.'

The blurry outline of Armen and his father stood across the room, arms crossed high against their chests. His mother slumped in a plastic chair. 'Property of Royal Canberra Hospital' came into focus.

His brother's eyes were as hard and mean as Vrezh had ever seen. *Don't say a thing*, Armen's look told him.

Vrezh didn't know what was going on. He hadn't expected to see Armen – or anyone – ever again.

'How does a barbecue just explode?' Their father paced the room, shouting, flinging his arms. 'We should sue the manufacturer, and this stupid friend of yours. Was *he* injured? Will *he* be here to take care of you?' The nurses told him to lower his voice.

Their parents hovered, their mother staying late each night, just as she did with Grandfather. After three days, their father returned to Sydney to reopen the jewellery store. Armen remained silent.

Vrezh didn't understand why he had survived.

After six days, the hospital released Vrezh. Painkillers kept his thoughts fuzzy, but the shame of adding to his mother's burden at home stabbed through his consciousness.

On Vrezh's first night back in his bedroom, Armen sent their mother to bed. 'I'll check up on him. And Grandfather.' She wavered, gave an exhausted nod, then kissed him on the cheek.

When she was gone, Armen set Vrezh's desk chair against his bed. He leant in, and Vrezh noticed the stubble that darkened his face. *Not right*, his brain told him. *Not right.*

'Why the fuck were you there alone?' That was Armen's opener.

Vrezh hadn't factored in the Rug King delivery van. That was how Armen got to him, the shed coming into view past the gum trees moments before the explosion ripped it apart.

His right hand ached, even though his hand, and everything below his bicep, was gone. Sliced almost clean through. Otherwise, aside from cuts and burns, he was surprisingly uninjured. The bomb was directional, like a claymore mine. Softie had positioned himself right in front of it. *Very convenient*, in Softie's words.

'What happened?'

'Looked like a hunk of metal tore through your arm. I wrecked my good belt making a tourniquet.' Armen's cologne wafted. 'Why were you there alone?'

'I don't remember,' Vrezh whispered.

'Softie call you up, tell you to come alone? He was fed up with you.' Armen shook his head. 'Thinking you're smarter than everybody and then you go blow yourself up.'

'I thought we would plan another shooting.'

'Because of Vaucluse? Softie wanted a bigger statement. We'd been planning a bombing there before that damn team came in for the assassination.'

Vrezh's shock pulled his eyes wide, dropped his mouth into an open O.

'But you were behind…'

Armen made as if to slap Vrezh, pulled back. 'Softie let you think that.'

The fog of Vrezh's mind rolled.

'Now I've got nothing!' Armen's voice was low but fiery. Spittle hit Vrezh's face. 'You think I want to spend my life cleaning carpets and listening to guys at the ARF argue about who spent three bucks on peanuts?'

He looked toward the door.

'I buried what was left of Softie, but you better hope no-one reported that explosion to the cops. I took care of things as much as I could.' He stood up, thrust the chair back toward the desk. 'Don't come to me again. We're done.'

*

Grey rain poured. A spring in the tollbooth seat prodded Vrezh's flesh. The endless stream of traffic marked off the months and then years he spent waiting for the police to come asking about Softie.

Still now, when he closed his eyes, he saw himself twisting the wires.

He wondered if some Turkish conspirator had ever contemplated killing Talaat. Wondered if it would have made any difference.

Vrezh had to believe it would have.

The ache in his right arm was constant. Phantom pain, the doctors called it.

He'd survived, but only in body. Armen ignored him, acted like he'd never had a brother. Even at their grandfather's funeral, he kept his distance.

When Armenia declared independence, Armen left within days. Vrezh felt his brother's absence like a cavity in his heart.

He never saw Armen again.

The rain battered the metal booth. The morning rush hour ended, and the traffic slowed, long minutes passing between vehicles. Tehlirian intruded on Vrezh's thoughts. He was back on Hardenbergstrasse, watching the tall, plain-faced Armenian head toward Talaat.

Vrezh risked a glance at his hero, then turned away, just another Berlin pedestrian in 1921, stepping onto a cross street or into a shop, never hearing the shot.

If there had ever been justice, it was a fluke, an aberration. It shimmered like a mirage, disappearing as Vrezh reached for it.

The Armenian alphabet monument on Mt Aragats depicts each letter of the unique alphabet.

Khachkars, intricately carved crosses, are an ancient Armenian tradition. The Peace Garden at NSW Parliament House features a khachkar memorial to victims of the Armenian genocide.

Republic Square, Yerevan

At Zorats Karer, 'Armenian Stonehenge'

Soviet apartment blocks in Yerevan

Essays

Writing Violence, Arousing Curiosity

Carmel Bird has described how, at times, a story's mechanism begins 'to tick away like a little clock' within her. I have experienced this myself. The novella *My Name Is Revenge*, however, was more like a scratch. Once the idea came to me, it scratched away at the inside of my heart with the persistence of a little clock. I had to write it, even though it scared me.

Although the characters are fictitious, I drew the plot from true events. The assassination of the Turkish consul-general and his bodyguard in Vaucluse, Sydney, in December 1980 was part of a series of international terrorist attacks. The Justice Commandos of the Armenian Genocide were a real group. They and similar groups committed dozens of acts of terrorism across Europe, the Middle East and North America, as well as in Australia, from 1973 to the early 1990s.

The details about the Sydney assassination, including the use of the Honda 500, the escape route, and the offer of a $250,000 reward all come from newspaper reports at the time. The assassins were never caught, though there are faint whispers in the Armenian Australian community about who they might have been. A second attack, a car bombing, took place in Melbourne in 1986. The bomb went off early, and only the bomber was killed.

Most Australians I meet don't know about these events, which isn't surprising. They seem to have faded from the news quickly. Likewise, I've met a lot of people who don't know anything about the history at the heart of this violence, the Armenian genocide of World War I. Or, if they've heard of it, they don't know much about it. I don't blame them – it's not like it's taught in school history classes. But they should know about it, in part because it's intricately linked with Australian history.

The Armenian genocide began on 24 April 1915. That this is the day before Anzac Day isn't a coincidence. The Ottoman government knew British forces were about to burst onto their shores, right near Constantinople, the capital. Feeling what historians have described as a 'state of siege', they decided to put into action the plans they'd laid to rid themselves of the Armenians. The Ottomans had come to see their Armenian citizens as an enemy, the reason their empire was crumbling. And so, during the long months of the Gallipoli offensive, some Anzac diggers were witness to the genocide. Some were taken prisoners-of-war and held in confiscated Armenian churches, while the Armenians were still being forced from their nearby homes. Some Anzac diggers were able to rescue Armenians. Their stories are preserved in war diaries and other documents at the Australian War Memorial, and now they're collected in *Australia, Armenia and the Great War* by Vicken Babkenian and Peter Stanley, published in 2016. Their stories deserve to be widely known. So why are they, and the genocide itself, so forgotten?

The Armenian genocide was part of the last gasp of the Ottoman Empire. By the time it ended, as many as 1.5 million Armenians were dead, and hundreds of thousands were stateless refugees, many of them orphans. They scattered around the world, to whatever communities would take them.

My great-grandparents were among those refugees. Paravon, my great-grandfather, had seen his entire family killed while he hid in the upper branches of a tree. He might have been as young as seven. We were never sure, because he didn't have a birth certificate. My great-grandmother Mariam was a little luckier, in that she didn't remember losing her family. She was only tiny, not old enough to even know her own name, when she was left with a trusted family while her own was herded out of town at gunpoint with the rest of the deportees, who would struggle through the desert toward what is now Syria, where, if they survived the journey with no food and little water, they would end up in concentration camps, or burnt alive or asphyxiated in caves.

When I interviewed my aunts and great uncles and second cousins, they all told slightly different versions of Mariam's story. In my favourite, the family friends who took her in were the local police chief and his wife. They were Turkish, of course. That's how she remained safe. A Turkish family took her in, risking their own lives. Perhaps it became too risky, because eventually Mariam ended up in an orphanage, the one where she met Paravon. They arrived in Canada as refugees in 1920.

As a child, I didn't know any of this. My dad grew up in one of Canada's Armenian communities, near Niagara Falls. His father was Armenian, but his mother was Polish, so he didn't speak Armenian at home. When he finished with school, he joined the Canadian military. I was born three provinces west, and we always lived at least 2000 kilometres away from dad's family.

I first learnt my great-grandfather's story when I was fifteen or so. Even then, I'd never heard of the genocide. My aunt told the story of how Paravon woke up in the middle of the night because he heard horses coming, so he climbed into a tree, where he saw his family and all the other Armenians in his village hung upside down from branches, their kneecaps sliced off so they would bleed to death as their homes burnt to the ground.

I've written about this for *Griffith Review*, and in a memoir about travelling through Armenia as a way of reconnecting with my family's history. But my great-grandparents weren't from what is the country of Armenia today. Today's Armenia is only a sliver of the lands where Armenians had lived since the time of Alexander the Great. Over the centuries, the Persian, Ottoman and Russian empires conquered and divided the traditional Armenian homelands, severing Armenians geographically and culturally. Today's Armenia had been part of Russian territory since the early nineteenth century, first under the Tsar, then again under Stalin and his Soviet cronies. My great-grandparents were from Anatolia, now eastern Turkey. Practically no Armenians live there today.

Armenians do travel there. I've interviewed Armenians who have gone to eastern Turkey to bring back a handful of soil from their father's or mother's village, sometimes to put on their parents' grave. I chose to travel in Armenia instead. I suppose I was nervous. Besides, I don't even know the names of the villages Mariam and Paravon came from. They died when I was very young. Now, no-one remembers details like that. No-one wrote them down.

When people hear about the Armenian genocide for the first time, they often comment on how similar it was to the Holocaust. This, again, is no coincidence. In World War I, Germany and the Ottoman Empire were allies. While the genocide was planned and orchestrated by the Ottoman government (the documents exist to prove it, as a brave Turkish historian named Taner Ackam has shown), German officers witnessed the genocide. A few became involved. Some of them had returned from German South West Africa, where they'd been involved in the genocide of the Herero and Nama peoples less than a decade earlier. The methods of the Holocaust – the train transport, the concentration camps, the propaganda portraying Jewish victims as dangerous bacteria – weren't Nazi innovations, but refinements of the methods used in the Armenian genocide. And as the wider world had largely forgotten the genocide by the 1930s, Adolf Hitler expected his own violence to fade into historical amnesia just as quickly. In 1939, days before the Nazi invasion of Poland, he connected the legacy of the genocide to his own violent political aspirations: 'Who today, after all, speaks of the annihilation of the Armenians?'

Even if Hitler hadn't definitively threaded these two histories together, it would be difficult to discuss the genocide without juxtaposing it against the Holocaust. This is not only because the genocide prefigured the Holocaust, but also because of their key distinction: the newborn Turkish government denied the genocide, and fairly successfully, as Hitler noted. Can you imagine if, after World War II, Germany denied the Holocaust ever happened? Of course they couldn't, you're saying. There was too much evidence. Too many people knew.

Just as many people knew about the Armenian genocide. *The New York Times* covered the story multiple times. It made the Australian news also, including *The Sydney Morning Herald* and *The Queensland Times* and *The West Australian*. Aid to Armenian survivors was the focus of the world's first international aid campaign. One of the campaign slogans really caught on, and for years after, when children across the Western world wouldn't finish their suppers, parents told them to 'remember the starving Armenians' (by the time I was child, the starving people we were remembering were Africans). The first international Red Cross mission provided aid to Armenians across the Near East. There were photographs, notably those taken by German soldier Armin Wegner, the negatives smuggled out in his belt. There was even an Australasian orphanage near Beirut that housed 1700 orphans, with milk, flour, honey, blankets and funding donated by Australians and New Zealanders. There were war tribunals that prefigured the Nuremberg trials. There were thousands of pages of evidence. Ottoman perpetrators were found guilty.

How does something so well known become forgotten? Easy. American advisors pointed out what was left of Armenia was nothing but rocks, and it didn't have oil. The remaining sliver of Armenian territory was sucked into the Soviet Union, where history began with Lenin. International attention turned elsewhere. Meanwhile, the hundreds of thousands of Armenian survivors scattered around the world didn't have a vocabulary to describe what they had experienced. They were refugees, trying to learn the languages of their new countries, trying to find work to support themselves, trying to have families and move on with their lives. They felt shame at their inability to protect their families and the loss of their homeland. They suffered survivor's guilt and PTSD. None of this was discussed at the time. The term 'genocide' and its legal framework were yet to exist: after learning of the annihilation of the Armenians, a Polish Jew and lawyer named Raphael Lemkin created the concept and dedicated his life to campaigning for both recognition of the term and international laws. It wasn't until Lemkin had lost more than forty members of his own family in the Holocaust that the United Nations adopted his suggested framework, which became the Convention on the Prevention and Punishment of the Crime of Genocide in 1948.

Germany didn't have a chance to deny the Holocaust, though the Nazis had started destroying documents before the war ended. The British and the Americans weren't going to let the German government rewrite history. Because of this, the Holocaust offers a model of what recognition could look like.

But after WWI, it was genocide deniers that formed the government of the newfound Turkish Republic. They have an international platform, and their ongoing denial isn't passive. The term 'Armenian genocide' is illegal in Turkey, and the Turkish government spends millions of dollars on its campaign to erase this violent chapter from its history. They insist on their rewritten, somewhat incoherent version, in which there were never any Armenians in Turkish territory, and even if there were, they killed many more Turks, so really Turks are the victims in all this. They fund academics in countries like the US to mould history to fit their narrative, exaggerating the importance of certain facts while ignoring others. This purposeful eradication of memory has been described as the final phase of genocide.

While the Turkish government is the driving force behind a century of genocide denial, it is also a major geopolitical player. Turkey is a strategic military partner of the US, which has two bases in Turkey. Not coincidentally, the US, the UK and Australia are among the countries that haven't recognised the genocide, though the European Union has. The US has tried, but every time the Turkish government threatens repercussions. Likewise, in *An Inconvenient Genocide*, Geoffrey Robertson notes that the UK Foreign Office described the Turkish government as 'neuralgic' on the subject of genocide recognition. Considering Turkey's political and commercial significance, the British government decided it was better not to upset them by acknowledging the truth.

You can see how there are injustices piled on top of injustices. Here's another: In 2018, Poland made it illegal to speak of Polish involvement in the Holocaust. As in Turkey, the Polish government seems to believe that silence will make their own uncomfortable history fade away. Yet the Polish government has officially recognised the historical fact of the Armenian genocide.

Israel, of course, is outraged about Poland's stance on the Holocaust. Fair enough. And of course Israelis feel solidarity with the Armenians, having suffered such similar and historically connected traumas, and Israel has long championed the international recognition of the genocide, right? Well, it's complicated.

There are many people in Israel, as well as Jewish Holocaust scholars and activists around the world, who are vocal about the importance of Armenian genocide recognition. In 2016, a sub-committee of Israel's national legislature announced its recognition of the genocide, noting the moral obligation to do so. Nationally, however, Israel has not officially recognised the Armenian genocide. As with the US, the UK and Australia, Israel is strategically allied with Turkey. And as with its other allies, Turkey puts intense diplomatic pressure on Israel to avoid mention of the genocide, and especially official recognition. In 2018, amid discussion of a possible federal debate regarding genocide recognition, *The Jerusalem Post* noted the response from Turkey's Foreign Ministry: 'We believe that the fact that Israel is placing the events of 1915 on the same level as the Holocaust will cause harm to Israel itself.'

In the years following the Holocaust, Turkey's international denial campaign created a rift with the one community that could have most intimately connected with Armenians in an effort toward mutual healing. Eminent Armenian historian Richard Hovannisian traces this back to Turkish efforts to create animosity between Armenians and Jews. As he writes, Turkish denialists 'uphold the truth and criminality of the Holocaust and make an appeal to keep it uncontaminated by confusing it in any way with the hoax of a so-called Armenian genocide.' Likewise, the imbalance in Western recognition of these two interconnected histories seems to fuel a strand of anti-Semitism I've encountered among some older Armenians. Denial ripples through communities in this way, from the geopolitical level to the personal.

This is all to say that Armenians have long been the underdogs of history. In the decades after WWI, the ongoing denial exacerbated the sense of rage and loss experienced not only by survivors but their children and grandchildren. For some, these feelings grew into frustration and disenfranchisement. Many Armenians feel persecuted. Can anyone blame them for wanting, even just for a moment, to take justice into their own hands?

A few of them did, of course, forming the Justice Commandos of the Armenian Genocide and targeting Turkish diplomats around the world. The Justice Commandos were the grandchildren of survivors. They wanted to ensure justice would happen while their grandparents were still alive to experience it. They wanted Turkey to acknowledge the genocide, to apologise and pay reparations. Political diplomacy had done nothing, and besides, it was the 1970s, so Armenia was still trapped under the boot of the Soviet Union, unable to voice its own opinions, unable even to tell its own history.

I'd been researching the genocide for years before I first learned about the Justice Commandos. Only a few history books mention these attacks, generally with a mere paragraph or two. I'd been so accustomed to reading about Armenians as victims, but now this handful of Armenian perpetrators – violent murderers – leapt off the page, shocking me. I couldn't condone or even empathise with their methods. And yet I understood their motives intimately. So the scratch began.

There isn't a great deal of Australian literature about the Armenian genocide. The only novels I'm aware of are Marcella Polain's *The Edge of the World*, Katerina Cosgrove's *Bone Ash Sky*, and to a lesser degree, Joan London's *Gilgamesh*. Each of these are startlingly unique and moving. My writing, I hope, will help keep the genocide alive in cultural memory, as these novels do. After all, this isn't just an Armenian story. In 2015, I attended an event in Sydney, where, on stage, the descendants of Australians who organised Armenian aid during and after WWI met descendants of genocide survivors. The Armenians gave the Aussies framed letters of thanks. Some of them hadn't known that their grandparents or great aunts or whoever had ever been involved in the humanitarian effort.

Maybe I should have written a gentle story about an event like that. But the *scratch, scratch, scratch* of the Justice

Commandos, their twisted logic – we will resolve violence with more violence – wouldn't leave me alone.

I challenged myself to find a way to write about this terrorism without condoning it.

Initially I planned to write from the point of view of a character like Armen, the more violent of the two brothers. Armen is utterly unconflicted. I tried to write my way into his perspective, but I couldn't relate to him. His thinking remained opaque to me, and so Vrezh stepped in to bridge the gap between my pacifist, artistic soul and Armen's hardline militancy. In this way, I've followed in the tradition of Kate Grenville's *The Secret River*, opting to use the 'less-violent' character device to contrast my protagonist's cautious, in some ways reluctant approach to violence with that of the more adamantly violent antagonists.

The word *vrezh* does mean revenge in Armenian, and some Armenian parents do name their children Vrezh. The scene in which Vrezh is made to drag the Turkish flag on the ground before burning it likewise comes from a tradition that still happens in Armenia. How would it feel to grow up with a name like Revenge, to be raised to hate because your family had been the victims of hate? I struggled to write Vrezh too, but I empathised with him.

I crafted Arshag, the grandfather, to provide insight into the brothers' motivations for violence, especially for Vrezh, who psychologically suffers his grandfather's trauma. He's also personally symbolic, as it was my great-grandfather, Paravon, whose story first made me aware of the genocide. Like the character of the grandfather, Paravon's memories of the genocide returned to him as nightmares after my great-grandmother died. For a time, nursing home attendants put him in a straightjacket. This is another way true events wove themselves into the novella.

As I continued to redraft the novella, I developed my understanding of how to imply violence in the narrative gaps, the spaces between details left for readers' imaginations to fill. In each draft, more of the grandfather's experiences of the genocide moved into the gaps. This can leave readers with a darker impression of the violence than detailed description can convey, while also not burdening them with excessive blood and gore on the page.

There was no question about setting the story in Australia. I'm fascinated by the Armenian Australian community. There are over 50,000 Armenians in Australia, most of who arrived here not immediately after the genocide, but from the 1950s on. Most didn't come from Armenia. More commonly, these families are twice dislocated, survivors of the genocide who settled in countries like Jordan, Lebanon, Iran, Iraq and Egypt and then, a generation later, came to Australia in search of security. Of course I wanted to emphasise the ties between Australian and Armenian history, as well as the historical similarities in the narratives of dispossession. Robert Manne has noted that in the creation of both Turkey and Australia, 'there was, for another people, a dreadful price to pay'. The histories of both countries 'have been burdened by the shadows cast by these events', he writes. In the novella, Vrezh alludes to this when he wonders about the Aboriginal people who might have once lived in the

NSW countryside. But he lacks the empathic imagination to connect their history to his own.

Another challenge was to ensure readers had enough historical context to understand the characters' motivations, but without overwhelming them with historical facts. There are many layers of history and geopolitics at play in these characters' lives. Over many drafts, my writers' group helped me strike a balance. I've strived to achieve that writerly feat of implying the iceberg by showing only its tip. I hope at least a few readers become more interested in this history, whether they want to know about the details of the assassination of Talaat Pasha in Berlin (it's an incredible story, well told in Eric Bogosian's *Operation Nemesis: The Assassination Plot that Avenged the Armenian Genocide*) or they become intrigued by the sweeping historical connections between not only the genocide and the Holocaust, but also with the Herero and the Nama people of what is today Namibia (in fact, Norman Naimark's *Genocide: A World History* convincingly connects the history of genocide from today's violence in Sudan back through the centuries to biblical times).

This is what I hope most for everything I write – that it arouses curiosity.

Armenian communities have an unhealthy relationship with the past. The novella focuses on Vrezh's struggle to reconstruct the Armenian cultural narrative in a way that, to his mind, achieves a sense of justice. He is working through the traumatic fragments of family memory in an attempt – however misguided – to develop a healthy relationship with the past, from which he and his community can move forward. My aim for this novella was not to mitigate responsibility for the international attacks committed by Armenian terrorists, but to honestly acknowledge this violence and the trauma that underlies it.

There are people in the Armenian community who, if they read this novella, might consider me a traitor to the Armenian cause. Some of them are people who have shaken my hand and encouraged me to write about the history. But they're not referring to the history of Armenians as perpetrators. Only as victims.

I guess it's no surprise that some people will always believe that best response to violence is more violence. As long as the 'right' people are suffering the violence, not themselves but their perceived enemies, violence is justified. But what did all the violence of the Justice Commandos and similar groups achieve? The Turkish government still denies the genocide. And now Turkish government officials can portray themselves as victims of Armenian terrorist violence, violence that took place in communities like Sydney's eastern suburbs.

Many Turkish people today do acknowledge the historical facts of the Armenian genocide, even though it remains illegal to do so in Turkey, a country not known for supporting free speech or civil rights. The Turkish historian I mentioned, Taner Ackam, has received death threats. He lives outside Turkey. Despite this atmosphere, 30,000 Turkish citizens signed a petition acknowledging the genocide and apologising for it in 2009. Their bravery echoes the actions of the Turkish family who sheltered my great-grandmother,

Mariam. Such resilience against hatred is another incredible story, and even now I feel the *scratch, scratch, scratch* on my heart. I will probably be writing about the Armenian genocide for the rest of my life, working to keep it alive in cultural memory, not only because it is part of my story, but because it is part of everyone's story.

Geghard Monastery, Armenia

Yerevan Railway Station

ԵՐԵՎԱՆ ԿԱՅԱ

Armenia became the world's first Christian nation in 301 CE.

Students perform a traditional dance on a football field in northern Armenia.

Tsitsernakaberd, Armenia's genocide memorial, Yerevan

The Crime of Crimes

The most intensely studied genocide is, without contest, the Holocaust. It's considered by some to be the archetypal genocide, a limit case, in part because the term genocide was first applied in a legal setting during the Nuremberg trials. Our ongoing interest in Nazi crimes against Jews and others seems unlikely to wane, particularly as new evidence is still being released. In 2017, the Weiner Library in London made public the UN War Crimes Commission archive, 900GB of evidence collected to prosecute Nazi government officials. It's a surfeit of documentation that could lead to the rewriting of aspects of Holocaust history.

Holocaust history is essential to our understanding of modern civilisation. Equally essential is the broader context of the Holocaust, its place within an historical continuum. The Holocaust can't be fully understood without the context of the Armenian genocide, which took place three decades earlier and provided the rough blueprints of modern extermination. And neither event can be fully understood without the context of the first genocide of the twentieth century, the German military's systematic attack on the Herero and Nama in colonial South West Africa.

Genocide as a term and a legal construct is a recent innovation. The United Nations adopted the Convention on the Prevention and Punishment of Genocide in 1948 – and this only happened, in large part, because of the efforts of one man, Raphael Lemkin. Lemkin was a Polish Jew and law student when he first learned about what was called the Armenian massacres. It baffled him that it was illegal for one man to kill another, yet there was no law against a government targeting its own citizens for destruction. In the 1920s, Lemkin dedicated himself to the study of what he came to label genocide. By the next decade, he found himself fleeing similar violence. Many of his family members died in the Holocaust.

Lemkin's story is full of such ironies. Another is that Lemkin came to understand genocide by studying its occurrence throughout human history; yet for decades after, cases of genocide were effectively siloed in their study. Only in recent years have genocide scholars returned to Lemkin's groundwork to consider this aspect of human civilisation from a broader historical perspective.

This is the approach Norman M Naimark takes in *Genocide: A World History*, part of the New Oxford World History Series that aims to 'investigate the total human experience'. Naimark began his career focused on modern Russian history, and after several books, turned his attention to crimes against humanity in *Fires of Hatred: Ethnic Cleansing in Twentieth-Century Europe*. His research has since centred on genocide, defined as acts committed with the intent to destroy identifiable groups, in whole or part. In *Genocide: A World History*, Naimark surveys humanity's capacity for this specific, brutal and pervasive crime.

Genocide is distinct from broader terms such as war crimes and crimes against humanity. In *Genocide: A World*

History, Naimark reviews cases of genocide dating to the ancient world, working through the warrior genocides committed by the Crusaders and the Mongols, to the Spanish conquest of the Americas, to what he terms the 'settler' genocides that occurred in North America, Africa and Australia. He draws a valuable connection between the paradigms that engendered settler genocides and the subsequent era of 'modern' genocides in Europe, including the Armenian genocide and the Holocaust.

Naimark also advocates for an expansion of the current UN definition of genocide to include Lemkin's original categories of social and political groups as victims; the current definition is limited to national, ethnical, racial or religious groups. Naimark stakes his argument for the broader definition on the unmistakable similarities in motives and strategies between genocides included under the current definition and communist, anti-communist and post-Cold War genocides. In doing so, he provides a comprehensive overview of genocide's development over the past three millennia. Genocides can differ significantly, varying in duration from days to decades, and in terms of their centralisation and the number of people involved. Regardless of these differences, Naimark concludes, 'there is a remarkable – indeed, frightening – similarity in genocidal violence over the past three millennia in human history.'

While some features of ancient violence – concubines, animal sacrifices and the salting of the earth – are now antiquated, the core characteristics of genocide remain: invoking ideologies and religion, political leaders agitate for the destruction of identifiable groups, resulting in armies of men killing noncombatants, including women and children. 'The killing is intentional, total, and eliminationist.'

We can trace this pattern to Western society's foundational histories. Naimark acknowledges that the Hebrew Bible is better viewed as a literary creation than an historical document; regardless of its factual accuracy, however, the Bible is fundamental to the Western discourse of elimination. In the Old Testament, the destruction of targeted identifiable groups was the will of God: 'Thou shall smite them, and utterly destroy them. ... Ye shall burn down their altars, and break down their images.' The recurrence of genocidal events in the Bible set precedents for future leaders to draw on. Likewise, whether the destruction of Troy depicted in Homer's *Iliad* and Virgil's *Aeneid* is historically accurate is not as important as the cultural impact of those texts.

In the thirteenth century, Mongol warriors used genocide as a military strategy, targeting some cities for complete destruction so others would submit without struggle. Across the Khwarezmian Empire, for example, the Mongols executed entire populations, with the exception of artisans and craftsmen. They destroyed culturally significant buildings, and left pyramids of skulls in their place. Mongol violence halved the population of Hungary in a single year.

The violence of the Crusaders likewise blurred into genocide, such as in the town of Béziers in 1204 CE, where the population was massacred under the mandate of Pope Innocent III. Catholic leaders present at the massacre wrote to the Pope: 'Our men spared no-one, irrespective of rank, sex or age, and put to the sword almost 20,000 people. After this great slaughter the whole city was despoiled and burnt, as Divine vengeance raged marvelously.'

Like the Mongols, the Pope used his legacy of violence to threaten others. In quoting a post-Béziers letter from the Pope to the people of Milan, Naimark parenthetically adds an exclamation mark: 'No multitude can resist the Lord of armies: leaving aside Old Testament examples [of extermination!] just as He recently subdued the heretics in Provence … so He has the power to reduce your city to nothing'.

Naimark provides only capsule summaries of case histories (the book is, in his own description, 'short, synoptic and selective'). The value of this broad perspective is in the compelling connections he makes, and his drawing out of the remarkable and frightening similarity in genocides throughout recorded history. In almost all the histories Naimark covers, there are two key motivating aspects for the perpetrators: a justifying ideology combined with promises of material gain – wealth, land, women, slaves. The Mongol massacres are a notable exception; eliminationist killing seems to have had no deeper ideological justification than as a means to power, unlike the 'holy war' of the Crusades or the religious and racial justification of the Spanish conquistadors.

The Spanish conquest of the Americas, which some scholars consider the most egregious case of genocide in human history, resulted in the deaths of up to 70 million people. While much of this was from disease, Naimark details how the harsh conditions of forced labour on the native populations created conditions that exacerbated the spread and efficacy of pathogens. The conquistadors' torture and murder of the natives 'reflected a deep-seated hostility to their victims' very existence as human beings'.

There is debate over whether this violence can be labelled genocide. The key question is whether the conquistadors had a mandate from the church or the court to destroy entire towns. Naimark concludes that the conquistadors 'operated in a framework that was created by the Spanish Crown'. Similarly, in what Naimark labels 'settler genocides' in North America, Australia and South Africa, the colonial powers hold ultimate responsibility for the exterminatory killings committed by settlers. Naimark highlights 'the deep paradox in a situation in which the new European arrivals attacked and sometimes eliminated the indigenous groups as inter-lopers.' In their racially based ideological system, European settlers were naturally entitled to these new lands, while 'inferior "small and dark" peoples, itinerant and ignorant, had no right to the land, even if they were to claim it in any formal way, which they often did not.'

In considering specific cases on each continent, Naimark draws distinctions between genocide and 'other forms of criminal discrimination'. He dedicates significant detail to the genocide of Tasmania's Aboriginal people, determining that their distinct groups can be regarded as 'a separate ethno-national unit' targeted for destruction by settlers with the support of the local government: 'They were killed by disease and by the deprivation brought on by colonial settlement. But they were also massacred in large numbers over a period of several decades.'

Understood on these terms, the nineteenth-century destruction of the North American Pequot and Yuki was likewise genocide, as was the extermination of the Cape San in South Africa. The treatment of the Cherokees, however, is better described as ethnic cleansing, as there was no intent to destroy this tribe. There are two clear similarities in each case of genocide: the settlers' conception of indigenous peoples as subhuman (the Yuki were referred to as beings 'who at least possess the human form') and the direct benefit of extermination to the settlers, namely the acquisition of land and, with it, the promise of wealth. Naimark points to the Old Testament imagery in the description of one settler who participated in an attack on the Pequot: 'Thus was God seen on the Mount ... burning them up in the fire of his Wrath.'

Technology engendered a sharp increase in the efficiency of mass killing in the twentieth century, the era of the modern genocide. Military forces could cover greater distances faster, communications technology enabled the immediate transmission of orders, and weapons became more efficient. Modern media enabled extremist politicians to spread more effectively the hate and fear of undesirable groups. And all this came about as nation-states forged their identities on nationalism driven in part by the pseudo-science of racial hierarchy. Here Naimark raises one of the key connections of the book, namely 'the important relationship between the racialist violence of settler genocide and the subsequent development of violent state ideologies and practices' that emerged in Europe.

The genocide of the Herero and Nama in German South West Africa marks this turning point. This was a settler genocide committed during the colonial era, but as Naimark notes, the involvement of the German state and army distinguishes it as the start of this new era of genocide. When the Herero rebelled against their treatment by German settlers in 1904, the German military attacked not only combatants, but also women and children. Their stated intent was the destruction of the native populations. The colony's German governor protested that killing the innocent natives was a waste of good labour, and after some time the military forces were withdrawn. The conditions of the governor's labour camps meant that they were, in reality, death camps and much of the population that had survived the military attacks died under German authority regardless.

Naimark notes the 'interesting and important linkages' between the events in German South West Africa and in the Ottoman Empire a decade later. The two cases of genocide are distinct, and to be clear, the Germans were not perpetrators of the Armenian genocide. Yet, because the Ottoman Empire and Germany were allies in the First World War, some German military officers did become directly involved in Ottoman actions against Armenian communities.

I began with the contention that it's difficult to fully understand the Holocaust without the context of the Armenian genocide. Most scholars of the Armenian genocide describe the violence of the final years of the Ottoman

Empire as prefiguring the Holocaust. Of course there are many differences in the details of these two grave historic events. But at a broad strokes level, it's the similarities that stand out, including the enactment of laws that targeted a reviled minority, the propaganda that compared that minority to infectious bacteria, the seizure of property, the use of train lines to transport victims, and the cold-blooded efficiency of government officials.

The most direct link between the Armenian genocide and the Holocaust was drawn by Adolf Hitler himself. In 1939, days before the invasion of Poland, the Nazi leader said in a speech to an assembly of his generals: 'Who after all speaks today of the annihilation of the Armenians?' Practically every history of the genocide references this quote, and it's even the subtitle of Geoffrey Robertson's legal and historical analysis, *An Inconvenient Genocide: Who Now Remembers the Armenians?*

Hitler's reference to the destruction of the Armenians is telling. As Naimark puts it, 'The Nazis were well aware of the Armenian genocide and of the general indifference of the world to the fate of the Armenians.' From the start of the genocide in 1915, headlines around the world detailed the horrors suffered by Armenians, with reports in papers from *The New York Times* to *The Age*. In the years immediately following the genocide, however, the rest of the world seemingly forgot Armenia, in part because its remaining territory had come under the control of the Soviet Union. Survivors were scattered around the world, and many fell silent. Aside from a handful of mostly inconsequential military tribunals led by the British in 1919, the Ottoman officials responsible for the genocide were never held accountable. Mustafa Kemel, also known as Ataturk, went on to establish the modern Turkish republic, and wove into its foundational myths the denial of any moral wrongdoing against any Armenians who may have once lived within its borders.

The assessment Hitler made in 1939 was accurate: the Ottomans had annihilated a minority population and gotten away with it. What was stopping the Nazis from doing the same thing? Peter Balakian includes a longer version of Hitler's quote in *The Burning Tigris: The Armenian Genocide and America's Response:* 'Genghis Khan led millions of women and children to slaughter – with premeditation and a happy heart. History sees him solely as the founder of a state. It's a matter of indifference to me what a weak European civilization will say about me. ... Who today, after all, speaks of the annihilation of the Armenians?'

The connection that Hitler makes between Mongol empire-building tactics, the annihilation of the Ottoman Armenians, and his own violent ambitions emphasises the importance of the work of Naimark and other genocide scholars. The genocidal policies of the Nazis were directed not only at the Jews, Naimark reminds us, but also at the Polish population, the Roma, the Sinti, homosexuals, and the mentally and physically disabled. And while the Nazi genocide is notable for the industrial methods of the gas chambers, 'the majority of Jews were executed in groups and buried in mass graves, a method that characterized genocide from its very beginnings.'

One of the main contentions of *Genocide: A World History* is that the definition of genocide should include the targeting of political and social groups. These groups were part of Lemkin's original definition of the term, but as a key member of the United Nations in 1948, the Soviet Union successfully argued for their removal from the definition. The USSR had committed genocide against its own populations, particularly during the Holodomor, the intentional starvation of the rural Ukrainian population that resulted in the deaths of as many as 10 million people. Naimark's previous book, *Stalin's Genocides*, explores Stalin's targeting of political groups for extermination in more detail. Under Lemkin's original definition, the mass starvation of China's Great Leap Forward and Pol Pot's violence against the Cambodian population likewise qualify as genocides.

Naimark explores ideological links between the Soviet, Chinese and Khmer genocides, while also considering the anti-communist genocides that marked the Cold War period. Similarly, anti-communist violence in Guatemala targeted entire indigenous communities as enemies of the government. In targeting the Mayans for destruction, the army destroyed the fields and burned the villages to ensure no-one would return. In Indonesia victims were likewise defined politically and targeted as such, both across the country and in 'potentially secessionist East Timor'.

It was only after the Cold War that the subject of genocide garnered international public attention. This came about through media coverage of three events: the war in former Yugoslavia that devolved into genocide; the Rwandan genocide, which could have been prevented by UN troops present in Rwanda at the time, if not for bureaucratic inaction; and the 1999 intervention in Kosovo. Despite the world's more sophisticated awareness of genocide, however, the Sudanese government used the army, police and paid militias to destroy 'rebellious' black tribes in 2003. Though the violence has since decreased, the Darfur region remains unsafe for black Africans; Sudanese President Omar al-Bashir, indicted for genocide, remains in power.

In each case history, Naimark summarises the circumstances that led to mass killing and discusses some of the debates around their categorisation as genocides. The book's broad scope and concise approach leaves little space to examine the wider contexts of any case. The ongoing Turkish denial of the Armenian genocide, for example, isn't mentioned. From one perspective, this is refreshing – the overwhelming historical evidence of the Armenian genocide, some of it provided by Turkish scholars examining Ottoman archives, has proven the fact of genocide. Noting the denial in some ways legitimises it. From another perspective, the denial of the genocide is a continuation of the genocide itself, and therefore worth addressing. Despite occurring a century ago, the legacy of the genocide and its denial still have significant geopolitical impact. It was only in 2016, for example, that Germany officially recognised the destruction of the Ottoman Armenians as genocide, predictably provoking the ire of the Turkish government.

The strength of *Genocide: A World History* is in Naimark's drawing out of the remarkable and frightening similarity in the cases considered. He dedicates significant detail to the use of rape as a strategy of war, and the gendered experience of victims. This emphasises one core aspect of the crime of crimes, which echoes on every page: genocide is never simply about killing. It is always accompanied by terrible violence – rape, torture, mutilation, the razing of entire communities. Throughout history, it has never been enough to 'simply' eliminate the dehumanised: they must be made to suffer.

I've studied and written about genocide for nearly a decade. My husband finds this interest morbid. Maybe this is a common perception. It came up immediately when I had the opportunity to interview Asya Darbinyan, a genocide scholar, at the Armenian Genocide Museum-Institute in Yerevan. 'When people hear you're studying genocide, they say, "Isn't it too depressing?" Of course it's sad when you read the details of how genocides were implemented,' she said. 'But you don't live it.'

A spirited, smiling woman in her late twenties, Darbinyan hoped to one day organise university forums 'to show genocide studies is not boring or only stressful'. Underpinning her enthusiasm was the sense that she was doing something important, even urgent. The Armenian genocide happened a century ago; few of its eyewitnesses are still alive today. But in studying its history, combatting its denial and sharing her work with others as a museum guide, Darbinyan had a powerful sense of vitality and exigency.

Considering the long history of genocide in the context of today's geopolitics and advances in digital capability should prompt a sense of urgency. Algorithms can now determine our political, sexual and religious orientations through our online activities. For advertisers, this is an opportunity. Juxtaposed with headlines such as those warning of Chechen plans to 'eliminate' the country's gay population, however, the opportunities become unsettling.

As *Genocide: A World History* makes clear, genocide has been driven by technological advances as much as any other area of human activity. Unless we come to better understand our capacity for genocide and address it openly and directly, there is no reason it won't continue to do so.

Celebrating the first day of school in northern Armenia

Life After Genocide

The discovery that I was racist came as a shock, as you might imagine. I'd just returned to Canada from several years in Asia and Latin America. I had a new job working with migrants, and I was volunteering with refugees. Like many Canadians, cultural diversity awareness campaigns had filled my childhood with posters featuring hands drawn in red, blue, purple, green – all linked in a perfect circle. I believed in those hands. I thought I was living their message.

And then I received an email from the coordinator of another program I volunteered with: 'I'm pleased to partner you with a lovely student from Turkey.' It felt like touching exposed wire. There was no way I would work with anyone from Turkey. I covered the computer screen in spittle. I was twenty-six. It had never occurred to me that those brightly-coloured, imaginary hands had no past to contend with.

Growing up as a dislocated military kid, shuffled across the Canadian prairies, I didn't think of myself as Armenian. My surname came from some strange, faraway land; it may as well have been Jupiter. It made sense that my surname could be one thing, and I could be something else. Sometimes my dad flew east, to visit his family, and returned with fruit leather, chewy grape-flavoured squares layered between cling wrap. 'My grandmother used to make this,' he'd say. Sometimes he'd make pilaf, a butter-soaked side dish I mistook for a type of rice. In fact, it's mixed with orzo.

Paravon and Mariam's wedding portrait, with Ashley and her father reflected.

When I was fourteen, my grandfather died. My parents and my sister and I went east together, to St Catharines, a sleepy retirement town on Lake Ontario, one of the Great Lakes. When the priest started speaking in a foreign language, I thought it was a mistake – he'd got the Kalagian funeral mixed up with someone else's. I was pretty sure nobody in my family spoke this discomforting language. In so many ways, I was struggling to make sense of the present. At that age, who's prepared for the crush of the past?

'When Paravon was eleven years old, in the small Armenian village where he lived with his family, he woke up in the middle of the night to the sound of approaching horses. He went outside and climbed into a tree to see what was happening. Turkish soldiers came into the village riding horses. They forced all the Armenians from their homes, including Paravon's family. He stayed in the tree, watching. The soldiers hung everyone upside down from their ankles in the trees. They cut off their kneecaps and left them to bleed to death. Then the army burned the village. Paravon stayed hidden. He was probably too scared to move. The soldiers left, but he remained there past sunrise, through the day, and into the next night. When he finally came down, he ran to a neighbouring village. Somehow after that he met Mariam. A few years later they ended up on a boat headed to Canada.'

I overheard my aunt tell my great-grandfather's story a few years later, at another family gathering. Paravon: the man we traced our surname back to. For me, his story destroyed that illusion some of us are lucky (or naive) enough to grow up with, the illusion that violence belongs to another, separate world. Its lack of context also unsettled me – I'd never heard of the Armenian genocide of World War I. Imagine learning that one of your relatives was packed into a cattle car to be hauled away and murdered in a state-run gas chamber if you'd never heard of the Holocaust.

Actually, it's difficult to imagine never having heard of the Holocaust. For better or worse, its cultural prevalence has led it to feature in films as unlikely as the 2011 Hollywood blockbuster *X-Men: First Class*. That film's opening ninety seconds depict mud-splattered labourers in black-and-white striped uniforms, working behind barbed fences, close-ups of ID numbers tattooed on withered arms, and the yellow Star of David on the chests of the arriving crowd. Throw in a few soldiers with rifles and it's almost unnecessary to have the caption 'Poland 1944' on the opening shot.

It's curious that many of us can identify the Holocaust from such scant details and yet know little or nothing about the Armenian genocide. Curious because the two events share eerily similar narratives of mass violence, railway cattle cars, dehumanisation and concentration camps. In fact, the Armenian genocide provided the blueprints for the Holocaust. In 1939, Adolf Hitler definitively threaded these two narratives together when he rationalised his 'final solution' for the Jews by pointing out that hardly anyone even remembered the Armenian genocide, let alone cared. His analysis was accurate. The genocide shattered Armenia so thoroughly that even its history broke apart, broke away from the wider world narrative of which it was an intrinsic part.

There is one key difference between the two histories: the government of Germany recognised their nation's role as perpetrator. The government of Turkey continues to deny theirs.

I've been researching this history for ten years now. At dinner parties and other gatherings, when asked what I do, I often mention it. My husband usually wanders off; he doesn't think genocide is an appropriate conversation topic at parties. Usually when he comes back, thirty or forty minutes later, he finds I'm still talking. One night he took me aside. 'You shouldn't go on too long – you don't want to bore people.' But I'm not the one pushing the topic. When people hear how similar the genocide is to the Holocaust, they struggle to understand why they know so much about one and nothing about the other. This is the power of Turkey's century of denial.

The genocide shattered Armenia, but the first cracks came centuries before, as warring empires split their communities. Armenians had lived across the Caucasus Mountains and Anatolian highlands for more than two thousand years. By the early 1900s, the borders of the Ottoman, Russian and Persian Empires had long separated them from each other.

The Ottoman Empire, the 'sick man of Europe', was in the midst of collapse, having lost much of its territory. The turbulent demise of the empire led to the search for a scapegoat. Partly because of their counterparts in Russia,

Armenians were cast as the Ottoman Empire's internal enemy. Propaganda campaigns depicted the Armenians as an 'invasive infection' in what was suddenly a nascent Turkish nation-state. (The Ottoman government also targeted Greeks and Assyrians, who faced similar fates to the Armenians. That these histories were studied separately until only recently is another symptom of the shattering that occurred at the end of the Ottoman era.)

On the eve of World War I, a Young Turks faction called the Committee of Union and Progress seized control of the empire. The political rallying call became 'Turkey for the Turks'. They aligned themselves with Germany, perceiving the war as an ideal situation for ending the 'Armenian Question.'

The genocide began with the arrest of two hundred and fifty Armenian religious, political and cultural leaders, which came just after midnight on 24 April 1915, as Anzac troops approached Gallipoli's shores. According to Robert Manne and others, this forthcoming attack (part of a state of siege inflicted on the Ottomans by the Anglo–French–Russian alliance) played a role in the Ottoman government's decision to execute the genocide. While the moral responsibility remains with the Ottoman government, this historical connection does make it unusual that there is little discussion of what some Anzac troops witnessed over the long months as combatants and prisoners of war in the Ottoman Empire. Some Australian researchers are now turning their attention to Anzac diaries and survivor accounts for evidence of the genocide. For example, in his diaries, now in the

Australian War Memorial, Australian solider Arthur James Mills describes helping Armenians escape the Turks, even carrying a four-year-old girl to safety on his camel.

Almost all of those arrested on 24 April were soon killed. The government's plans then proceeded swiftly: military police arrived in town after town, ordering Armenian men into military service, then executing them a few kilometres away. They rounded up women, children and the elderly, and ordered them 'deported.' Allowed to bring only what they could carry, these civilians were marched into isolated, barren regions to die of starvation and exposure. Some marched for weeks with little food or water. Many were kidnapped and sold into slavery or 'Turkified' – forced to convert to Islam and serve in Turkish homes. Along the Black Sea, soldiers took thousands by the boatful to be drowned. They packed Armenians into cattle cars on the newly built railway to expedite the deportation. Concentration camps in the Syrian Desert held as many as forty thousand Armenians. This is where a rudimentary form of the gas chamber as a tool for mass murder was trialed. Those who had survived the death marches were packed into caves, where fire smoke filled their last breaths.

The numbers vary, but at least a million Armenians died. If not directly involved, German officers serving in Ottoman territory were witness to the genocide. England, France and Russia described the attacks on Armenians as crimes against humanity – the original use of the phrase.

When I learned this history as a teen, the roles established in Paravon's story held: perpetrator, denier and villain against victim, hero and human. These roles weren't confined to the past. When the Canadian government recognised the genocide through legislation in 2004, Turkey withdrew its ambassador in protest. The tactics had changed; the intent hadn't.

It would have been 1915 or perhaps 1916 when Paravon witnessed his family killed. Mariam had been separated from her family. Was it easier or harder for her, keeping up hope that someone might have survived? For the rest of her life, whenever she met fellow Armenians, she would ask if they had known anyone from her village in Erzurum, if they had heard anything about her family.

It was a small miracle that the couple made it into Canada in 1920. Although not quite as ironclad as Australia's immigration policies, Canada's legislation at the time labelled Armenians 'Asiatics' and therefore undesirable. As Isabel Kaprielian-Churchill describes in *Like Our Mountains*, Paravon and Mariam would have needed $250 each as 'landing money' – and a relative to support them. By luck, Paravon had an uncle who'd come to Canada for work before the genocide, before immigration laws crashed down like a steel gate. How they managed to track each other down – Through Near East Relief? Through the League of Nations? – and how the uncle managed to obtain visas for the couple remain mysteries, like so much of Paravon's early life.

Once safely inside Canada's expansive borders, Paravon and Mariam settled into domesticity and hard work. Like most Armenian men in St Catharines, he took a job at

McKinnon Dash and Metal Works, which was later absorbed into General Motors and is now a defunct factory in the midst of the city. Paravon worked in the foundry, relying on co-workers to translate. The couple had six children. They bought a little farm and grew fruits and veggies. Despite her illiteracy, Mariam became a bit of a local real estate baroness. Later in life, she gifted a property to each of her children. Like so many survivors, theirs is a story of resilience.

After I received the coordinator's devastating email, I schemed to back out of my volunteering commitment. But eventually I did meet the Turkish student, who was as smiling and warm and thoughtful as the coordinator has assured me. We soon became good friends, and her mother shipped me a set of tiny Turkish coffee cups and a copper pot. On the Canadian prairies, she taught me to make gritty, heady Turkish coffee heaped with sugar. It was a tradition Mariam and Paravon would have recognised as Armenian – but one that I still didn't.

Three generations down, my Armenian genes were mixed up with Irish, Scottish and Polish ones; culturally I felt as bland as a wheat field. But my sharp, visceral reaction to the news of the Turkish student made me wonder if there was some essential Armenianness inside me, a few drops of pomegranate juice in my veins.

After my Turkish friend returned to Ankara, I travelled to St Catharines. I worried my father's family would find my desire to understand them as Armenians an odd request, voyeuristic even. But they dug dusty photo albums out of their attics and rang up sharp-witted, white-haired ladies of my grandfather's generation. Paravon and Mariam had been gone nearly thirty years. Of their six children, only one was still alive.

I met Mariam and Paravon once. In the orange-tinted photo, I'm clad in frilly infant clothes, cuddled on Mariam's lap on a jungle-print couch. With their sun-worn skin, Mariam and Paravon look like they've stepped out of a much older, much different world. Mariam, broad and hearty, has a pinched smile and bright eyes. Paravon, his wooden cane resting beside him, looks ancient.

After the genocide, refugees carried shards of their Armenian lives around the world. Huddled near McKinnon Dash and Metal Works, the growing Armenian community in St Catharines attempted to reconstruct what they could. Paravon and Mariam helped to build the first Armenian church in Canada, St Gregory the Illuminator. Mariam learned to cook traditional dishes and desserts from older Armenian women – she'd been too young to have learned much, if anything, when she lost her mother. The community ran an evening school to teach language and culture. All my grandfather's generation attended, and some of my dad's generation as well. But when it came time for my dad to attend, the momentum was lost. The school closed. My dad never learned Armenian, and Paravon's English was limited. Theirs was a relationship of tractor driving and fruit picking. Armenians have a term for this process of lost identity over generations in the diaspora – they call it white genocide.

*

The smell of butter filled the kitchen when I visited my dad's cousin, Laura. It wafted from a pot on the stove, where a layer of whitish murk floated atop silky yellow butter fat. Laura demonstrated how to layer paper-thin sheets of filo dough into a glass pan and brush them with the butter. Teaching me to make pakhlava included teaching me to pronounce it as Mariam would have, in Western Armenian, exchanging the rounded b for a softer p. The east/west, Russian/Turkish split between dialects is one of many rifts between Armenia and its far-flung diaspora.

Armenian Cooking Today, a worn red binder of recipes, lay open on the bench. 'Today' referred to 1975. While I brushed butter, Laura leafed through another cookbook, this one stuffed with handwritten recipes from Mariam (transcribed by her daughter and other culinary confidants). The names weren't appealing – boereg, bourma, kufteh – but the dishes sounded delectably offbeat: cheese-stuffed pastry, pakhlava on a stick, meatballs of ground steak and pine nuts. A typical instruction: 'Add enough flour to have texture like an earlobe.' Recipes featured titles such as 'Pilaf for 100 people.' In Mariam's day, there was always a church picnic or community feast to prepare for. Laura also had the recipe for bastegh, the famous fruit leather my dad used to bring home from his solo visits to St Catharines. After boiling down the fruit, the syrupy remnants have to be spread flat on muslin sheets and hung to dry for days.

Laura recalled Mariam making her own filo dough. Ours came from a box. The near-translucent pastry requires time, space and patience, and Laura was a mother and career woman. Who could blame her for finding shortcuts to Armenianness?

That smell of softly bubbling butter mingled with hints of garlic when I received another cooking lesson from Richelle, Laura's sister. This pot held more than one kilogram of melted butter, a heart-stopping ocean. We were making pagarch, a traditional dish usually reserved for Christmas; my September visit was an exception. Pagarch was tied up with family memories of Paravon, who joined in its preparation for the Armenian Christmas celebration on 6 January. While the women did almost all the cooking, the men's involvement in pagarch stood out as an exception for the pragmatic reason that kneading the massive amount of dough required a lot of physical strength. For years, the men of the St Catharines community made it on the stage at the church, the only place with sufficient space to knead a pagarch large enough for the shared Christmas feast. No-one kneaded pagarch on the church stage anymore. Scaled-down versions of the brown bread wheel came from a Toronto bakery. We sliced the crust off the top of our fifteen-centimetre-wide pagarch bread and dug the insides out with a spoon, creating crumbly mounds. Heaping these back inside the crust, we poured the melted butter and a garlic yogurt soup overtop – a reverse volcano.

For my family, pagarch is quintessentially Armenian, something made in memory of Mariam and Paravon, a surviving token of a time and place before genocide. But many Armenians have never heard of it. Likely it was a regional dish from Keghi, where most Armenian migrants

Pagarch in September

Village traffic, Armenia

Soviet debris, rural Armenia

Yerevan market

to St Catharines were from. No-one really knows. It's among what was lost in the genocide: lives, livelihoods, land, homes, businesses, cultural heritage, answers.

White genocide could describe much of my family, even those still living in St Catharines. Few still speak that consonant-heavy language I first remember hearing at my grandfather's funeral. Few still attend church services. The religion and the language, the foundations of Armenian culture, are now almost gone. Richelle and Laura are famous in the community for their Armenian culinary prowess: Richelle does the savoury dishes, Laura the desserts. But so far, among their kids – my generation – there's no passion to make the dishes Mariam fed her family with. St Catharines is a retirement community with an ageing population. As has happened in other nearby cities, the Armenian community is fading away. St Gregory the Illuminator still stands across the street from the now-defunct GM factory, in danger of ending up just as empty.

Descendants of genocide survivors wanting to trace back their ancestral roots have two choices. They can go to eastern Turkey, where there may or may not be traces of their family's villages. There may be an Armenian church that is now a mosque, or a barn, or just rubble. They may find people eager to help them, or they may find themselves unwelcomed. What they won't find, in eastern Turkey, is Armenian culture.

Even if I'd wanted to go to Turkey, the names of the villages where Mariam's and Paravon's lives began had been lost since their deaths. I chose to visit Armenia instead. Though the pocket of Armenia that remains today is a remnant from the Russian Empire, it's the closest cultural torchbearer of the lives Paravon and Mariam might have lived.

I arrived expecting to feel the genocide's long shadow. This was where many refugees had fled, where the orphan army had deterred Ataturk's military forces – slowed them down at least, until the Russians came in and declared the whole place Soviet in 1920. Armenians in Armenia have had to move on, not because the genocide's legacies are any more settled there, but because of a relentless series of new crises: poverty, starvation and purges under Stalin; Soviet cultural takeover; a devastating earthquake; and a war with Azerbaijan that left most of the country without electricity or gas for much of the 1990s. One could argue, however, that the root of many of these events reaches back to the genocide.

Today, rusting Soviet detritus litters the landscape – truck carcasses, abandoned factories, Ferris wheels. Outside the capital, there's often more cow traffic than car traffic. Women aren't allowed to drive. Some regions are verdant, covered by apricot and pomegranate orchards. But many regions are so mountainous and rock-strewn that even the imagination falters – how is it possible to live in such a place? The answer for many Armenians is that it's not. Independent since the collapse of the USSR, Armenia suffers mass unemployment, endemic corruption and widespread poverty. It's lost a quarter of its population since independence. Only three million people remain in Armenia, compared to as many as eight million in the diaspora.

I travelled all across the country, tracing the ancient silk caravan roads. Once I learned the 'correct' pronunciation of my surname (kah-lah-*jyan*, not the anglicised kah-*lay*-gin I'd used all my life) Armenians welcomed me with open arms. Toward the end of my sweaty, dusty summer in the Caucasus, I discovered what I'd been searching for all along.

'In my hostel, they told me I am the first Turk to stay there. I've heard this everywhere!' Başak said, her hands fluttering around her like birds as she spoke. I encountered Başak by chance outside Yerevan's train station, the day before her return to Istanbul. In her early thirties, with a wide, distinctive face, deep-set dark eyes and an athletic figure, she was travelling solo in Armenia to speak with people as her way of acknowledging the genocide.

'This trip, I am only staying three days. I like it here. I would come again. But it was difficult to get the visa. Some people I meet, when I say I am Turkish, the conversation stops. They are not bad to me, no-one is bad to me, but the conversation stops.' It relieved me to know she'd been treated decently, though by this time I understood that in Armenia, anger mostly focused on Azerbaijan, thanks to the recent war – yet another rift with the diaspora. In contrast to Başak, an Azerbaijani wouldn't have received an entry visa.

'Here I feel uncomfortable and guilty, and some people seem irritated by me. This is the first time I've felt uncomfortable about my nationality, and I've travelled all over Europe.

But I came to speak to Armenians, to see how they're feeling, and to see the land, the people's faces. When I'm with people, I can see it in people's eyes, and people's eyes cannot lie.' In this way, Başak had also come to confirm what she'd learned about the genocide.

In high school, Başak learned Turkey's rewritten narrative of the Turkish–Armenian 'civil war' – just like my Turkish friend in Canada, who, when I finally asked her about it, told me gently that the Armenian claim was a lie.

'Gradually, more and more people recognise it and talk about it. In the early 1990s, no-one talked about it. My mother tells me, "You will go to prison."' Başak was familiar with jail, having already spent one night there after a protest. She was yet one more victim of her government's policies.

Başak had also broken up with a long-term boyfriend after he tried to prevent her from attending a protest for genocide recognition – a century after the fact and still there was this struggle. It had worked its way under our skin, like a sliver of glass. I shared my story, about the email and how angry I'd felt, and how ashamed that made me. My journey had started in cowardice, hers in bravery. We'd come from opposite directions to arrive in the same place.

When I said goodbye to Başak, I confirmed I couldn't use her real name. 'I want you very much to use my real name, but this' – recognising the genocide – 'is a crime in Turkey. I'm not enough rich to immigrate to another country.'

In the decades following the genocide, there were no official commemorations or acknowledgments. With a few

Paravon and Mariam with their great-granddaughter, Ashley, circa 1984 (photo credit: Gary Kalagian)

million Armenians facing starvation in the Soviet Union, and hundreds of thousands scattered in orphanages, refugee camps and budding, far-flung communities in foreign countries, Armenians had no context for creating public memory and awareness. The USSR suppressed talk and reactions to the genocide. In the history museum they eventually built in Yerevan, Armenia's capital, history began with the Russian revolution.

Armenians struggled under a burden of shame. The resulting silence lasted until 24 April 1965, the genocide's fiftieth anniversary. That day, public commemorations spontaneously broke out in Armenia, Moscow and Beirut, at the United Nations, and across the United States. In Armenia, the commemoration turned to a protest. Demands led first to the Tsitsernakaberd Memorial in 1967 and much later, in 1995, to the accompanying museum, situated on a hilltop in Yerevan.

Even after those first public commemorations, there was little public discussion of the genocide. Into the 1990s, victims who spoke out risked stigmatisation and humiliation. I might have found this silence difficult to imagine, except that it was one of Paravon's infamous attributes. Even with Armenian speakers, he was taciturn. If his grandchildren rang while Mariam was out, he would answer 'Mama not home!' and hang up. Paravon's silence was juxtaposed with an explosive temper. He'd get so angry he would stutter, hollering at Mariam. By all accounts, she took this in stride.

The Armenian history of trauma has gone largely unacknowledged and undiagnosed. In *Consequences of Denial*,

Aida Alayarian details the psychological effects of the Turkish denial on Armenians. She describes silence itself as a further kind of trauma, adding another layer of psychological distress. Additionally, when trauma is experienced on a mass scale and left unaddressed, it passes on to the next generation, who may suffer similar psychological effects with no ability to express their origins. I suspected this might explain the volatile temper that ran in my Armenian family.

Despite his occasional explosiveness, Paravon was loving, especially toward Mariam. The two always looked at each other like newlyweds. Whatever had brought them together, their obvious love left an impression on their family. When they both ended up in a nursing home, Paravon would sneak into Mariam's bed.

Mariam died first. It seemed to be the second great tragedy of Paravon's life. He was incapable of processing it. 'He wouldn't believe it,' one of his granddaughters said. When the family took him to the funeral home to see Mariam in her coffin, he shouted at her, demanding '*Eli*, Mariam, *eli!*' Get up! But she didn't get up, so he became convinced it wasn't her. He told people she'd run off with another man and accused his sons of being in conspiracy with her, of orchestrating this show.

After losing Mariam, Paravon started having hallucinations, waking versions of the nightmares he'd suffered all his life, terrifying visions of Turks coming to kill him, of sabres stabbing upward through tree branches. He raved about it, experiencing the horror of his childhood all over. In the last weeks of his life, his screaming fits became so severe, the nursing home staff restrained him with a straight jacket. He died not long after Mariam.

Though it took a few decades after the genocide, Armenians became part of Australia's cultural milieu as well. After immigration laws changed, an influx of Armenians migrated from communities in Jordan, Iran, Egypt, Lebanon and many other places of instability. Their family narratives contain layers of dislocation. I ended up in Sydney as well, and found myself drawn to the Armenian community. As an *odar* – an outsider – I see them all as Armenians. They see each other differently, marking out the distinctions. Perhaps a culture, once shattered, remains so. Still, I see in Sydney the community vitality I imagine existed in St Catharines when Paravon and Mariam were raising their six children: Armenian Saturday schools and church feasts, Armenian magazines and radio shows, art exhibitions and sporting events.

Just as Canadian Armenians succeeded in convincing their government of the importance of standing up to genocide denial, Australian Armenians work toward having the genocide federally recognised. The political relationship with Turkey makes it more challenging, but now that the Anzac centenary has passed, Australian Armenians have hope that their government will find the moral courage to call out and counteract racist intent.

For years, I wondered what caused my own faltering into racism. Perhaps I'd tuned into a background frequency among my Armenian family, just below the volume of consciousness. But when I interviewed my family, nothing supported this theory.

When I finally spoke to my aunt again, the one who first shared Paravon's history, I discovered a key fact – another splinter of the story. Had I learned it when I was young, it might have changed the way Paravon's story took seed in my brain.

'Mariam was saved by the love of a Turkish family. They risked their lives to shelter her. Because of them, she always spoke of kindness. She never allowed a single bad word.'

Norovank Monastery, Armenia

Acknowledgments

My parents have supported my writing since my first story appeared in *Young Saskatchewan Writers*, when I was seven. My most heartfelt thanks goes to them. My husband began as my sketch comedy cowriter back in 2003, and has supported me in more ways than even an accountant could track. And way back in 2009, my in-laws gifted me a stack of Armenian history books to get this ball rolling. Each of these people also read drafts of the novella and gave feedback, and I can't thank them enough.

I owe sincere thanks to many people who have helped me along the way, including the extended Kalagian clan, who generously shared their homes, memories, photos and recipes with me when I first began researching my Armenian heritage in 2010, including Bernice Kalagian, Mary Anne Jablonski, Diane Creamer, Trisha Jones, Richelle and Andrea Leahy, Laura Hoogasian Klimek, Robyn Stewart, Richard Hoogasian, Richard and Judy Kalagian, Carol Kalagian, Nancy Kalagian-Nunn and Dixie Petti. Likewise, an incredible number of people in Australia's Armenian community have shared their stories with me, including most notably Ani Galoyan and her family. In Armenia, I was welcomed with open arms everywhere I went. To the many Armenians, American Peace Corps volunteers and others in Armenia who offered immense kindness and guided my understanding of Armenian heritage, culture and history

– thank you. Thank you as well to the Turkish friends who have graciously spoken with me.

So many people have provided kindness, support and guidance, and to each of them I'm forever grateful: the incredible Writing NSW staff, Jane McCredie, Julia Tsalis, Jeanne Kinninmont, Sherry Landow, Cassie Watson, Bridget Lutherborrow, Aurora Scott, Dan Hogan, and our many fabulous interns including Suzi 'Sirius' Ferré, Claire Bradshaw, Eliza Auld and Cathy Bouris; my amazingly talented writers' group, Andrea Tomaz, Andrew Christie, Gabiann Marin, James Watson, Simon Veksner, Jonathon Shannon, Amanda Ortlepp, and especially Michelle Troxler and the generous and talented Jacqui Dent; the publishers and editors who have supported my writing, especially Linda Funnell and Jean Bedford, Julianne Schultz and Jerath Head, Rebecca Starford and Hanna Kent, Kirsten Krauth, Catriona Menzies-Pike, Stephen Romei, Paul Ham, Zoe Norton Lodge and Ben Jenkins; my academic advisors, especially Marcelle Freiman and the Macquarie University English Department, and Jane Park; the utterly inspiring Ren Arcamone; Hanna Kivistö, in whose unmatchable company I first forged a writing practise; Marije Nieuwenhuis, provider of early and incisive feedback; my fellow KSP writing fellows, Christine Scuderi and Nicole Hodgson; Fran Giudici, the best fan any writer could ask for; Lindsey Wiebe, for her unflagging support and steadying friendship; Kerry and Janet McLuhan; Helena Klanjscek, Carol Neuschul, Fran Jakin, Rachel Ramberran and Sarah Hodges-Kolisnyk; my many incredible teachers and mentors, including Felicity

Castagna and Toni 'The Unpredictable Plotter' Jordan, who both gave feedback on this novella, Luke Ryan, Claire Scobie, Maxine Beneba Clarke, Mishi Saran, Ethan Gilsdorf, Irene Lemon and Armin Wiebe; the inestimably supportive Walter Mason; and my fellow writers, who are a constant source of inspiration and encouragement, including Lee Kofman, Arna Radovich, Eva Lomski, Robin Riedstra, Sharon Livingston, Rebecca Chaney, LA Larkin, Adele Dumont, James Fry, Inga Simpson, Katherine Howell, Graham Wilson and Wai Chim.

And finally to Bronwyn Mehan and the Spineless Wonders team, Carmel Bird, State Library Victoria and Tablo, for bringing *My Name Is Revenge* into the wider world through the inaugural Carmel Bird Digital Literary Award – my immense thanks.

Bibliography

Akçam, T. 2006 *A Shameful Act: The Armenian Genocide and the Question of Turkish Responsibility*, Metropolitan Books/Holt, New York.

Alayarian, A. 2008 *Consequences of Denial*, Karnac, London.

Arlen, M.J. 1976 *Passage to Ararat*, Chatto & Windus, London.

Babkenian, V. and Stanley, P. 2016 *Armenia, Australia and the Great War*, NewSouth, Sydney.

Balakian, P. 2003 *The Burning Tigris: The Armenian Genocide and America's Response*, HarperCollins, New York.

Bird, C. 2015 *My Hearts Are Your Hearts: Twenty New Stories and Their Origins*, Spineless Wonders, Sydney.

Bogosian, E. 2015 *Operation Nemesis: The Assassination Plot that Avenged the Armenian Genocide*, Hachette, Sydney.

Grenville, K. 2005 *The Secret River*, Text, Melbourne.

Hovannisian, R. (ed) 1999 *Remembrance and Denial: The Case of the Armenian Genocide*, Wayne State University Press, Detroit.

Hovannisian, R (ed). 2003 *Looking Backward, Moving Forward: Confronting the Armenian Genocide*, Transaction Publishers, New Brunswick, NJ.

Kaprielian-Churchill, I. 2005 *Like Our Mountains: A History of Armenians in Canada*, McGill-Queens University Press, Montreal.

Kirkland, J. 1980 'The Social Adjustment of Armenian Immigrants in Australia', *International Migration*, 21.4, 515-39.

Kirkland, J. 1980 'Armenian Migration, Settlement and Adjustment in Australia', *International Migration*, 22.4, 101-28.

Kissane, A. 2008 '"The Gun Went Off": Teaching the Writing of Violence', *TEXT*, 12.2, October.

Manne, R. 2007 'A Turkish Tale: Gallipoli and the Armenian Genocide', *The Monthly*, February, online.

Moorehead, A. 1959 *Gallipoli*, Arrow Books, London.

Naimark, N. 2017 *Genocide: A World History*, Oxford University Press, Oxford.

Power, S. 2002 *"A Problem from Hell": America and the Age of Genocide*, Basic Books, New York.

Robertson, G. 2015 *An Inconvenient Genocide*, Random House, Sydney.

Sands, P. 2016 *East West Street: On the Origins of Genocide and Crimes Against Humanity*, Wiedenfeld & Nicholson, London.

Previous Publications

'The Crime of Crimes' was first published by *Sydney Review of Books*, August 2017.

'Life After Genocide' was first published by *Griffith Review*, July 2015.

Old Khndzoresk, abandoned cave village
(photo credit: Lyndsay Leahy)

Biography

Ashley Kalagian Blunt's writing appears in *Griffith Review*, *Sydney Review of Books*, *Westerly*, *The Australian*, *The Big Issue*, *Kill Your Darlings* and more. Her non-fiction work *Full of Donkey: Travels in Armenia* was shortlisted for the 2018 Impress Prize and the 2017 *Kill Your Darlings* Unpublished Manuscript Award.

Ashley has appeared at Story Club, Little Fictions, Noted Festival and the National Young Writers' Festival, and is a Moth StorySLAM winner. Before moving to Australia, she lived and worked in Canada, South Korea, Peru and Mexico.

In 2012, she spent two months travelling in Armenia and interviewing people throughout the country. Unless otherwise noted, photos are hers.

Find her at **ashleykalagianblunt.com** and on Facebook, Twitter and Instagram @AKalagianBlunt